G R JORDAN

Drop Like Flies

A Highlands and Islands Detective Thriller #42

People around me die. They drop like
flies. I've gone through life leaving a
trail of dead bodies behind me.

ILONA ANDREWS

Contents

Foreword

The events of this book, while based around real and also fictitious locations around Scotland, are entirely fictional and all characters do not represent any living or deceased person. All companies are fictitious representations and locations have been modified for the purposes of the story. This novel is best read while accompanied by an attractive but deadly black haired secret agent!

Acknowledgments

To Ken, Jean, Colin, Evelyn, John and Rosemary for your work in bringing this novel to completion, your time and effort is deeply appreciated.

Books by G R Jordan

The Contessa Munroe Mysteries (Cozy Mystery)

1. Corpse Reviver
2. Frostbite
3. Cobra's Fang

The Patrick Smythe Series (Crime)

1. The Disappearance of Russell Hadleigh
2. The Graves of Calgary Bay
3. The Fairy Pools Gathering

Austerley & Kirkgordon Series (Fantasy)

1. Crescendo!
2. The Darkness at Dillingham
3. Dagon's Revenge
4. Ship of Doom

Supernatural and Elder Threat Assessment Agency (SETAA) Series (Fantasy)

1. Scarlett O'Meara: Beastmaster

Island Adventures Series (Cosy Fantasy Adventure)

1. Surface Tensions

Dark Wen Series (Horror Fantasy)

1. The Blasphemous Welcome
2. The Demon's Chalice

Chapter 01

'Who in their right mind comes out on a day like this?'

'You have to golf in all weathers. Can't be one of these part-time golfers,' said Ian.

'Part-time golfer?' said Murdo. 'Part-time course, more like. Where do you think we are? Augusta?'

'The way you play, Murdo, it's more like crazy golf.'

'Did you even see any of that fairway in the last one?' said John, another of his playing partners.

'It's nothing ever but crazy golf out here. That wind's coming in, too.'

The golf course on the Isle of Barra was certainly not the Augusta National, home of the US Masters. But then again, the weather was never Augusta-like either. The idea of growing a large bunch of azaleas behind one of the greens had never occurred to Murdo, and probably never would.

What did occur to Murdo was he was currently six feet from the hole and had a putt to win the hole. They were on the second hole, soon to go to the third tee box, over by the rocks. The green was rather rough and ready, but then again, so was the weather out here. There was no full-time course management. They did well just to be able to play.

The Isle of Barra, at the southern end of the Outer Hebrides, wasn't a large island, and the three golfers knew each other well. They also knew that they had to get out early that morning, for a storm was whipping up. There was an increase in the wind that was already being felt, and Murdo wondered if they'd get round nine holes in time to get back inside for a decent cup of tea.

'How did you stick that one so close?' said Ian. Ian's ball was lying off the green, close by a rock. He eyed up the shot he would have, withdrew a pitching wedge from his bag, and addressed the ball.

'Come on, Ian,' said John. 'Freezing out here.'

'There's the southern softy again,' said Murdo. 'You take your time, Ian. You do whatever you need to do. You're not getting close anyway.'

Ian looked up and swore at Murdo. 'Can we have a little bit of calm, please? Quiet. You wouldn't get this sort of nonsense playing at Augusta, would you?'

'You wouldn't get to play at Augusta, not unless you got a different job and earned a heck of a lot of money.'

'You certainly wouldn't qualify.'

'Shush,' said Ian, and Murdo halted his lambasting for a moment. Ian swung the club head back, raced in behind the ball, but came in about a half inch too early. He hit the turf and the ball flopped forward about two feet. Murdo burst out laughing, almost doubling over in the process.

'Augusta is safe,' said John.

'Shut up,' said Ian. He stepped forward quickly, took a quick swing at the ball, and clipped it up onto the green, leaving it some twelve feet from the hole. 'Don't know why I bother.

Take more time over it and you just get worse.'

'Speed golf. Is that it?' said John. 'You need to be doing speed golf. Bit like speed dating.'

'No, that's Murdo,' said Ian. 'Murdo's the speed-dating man. Did you see him the other night?'

Murdo looked up, his eyes raised, ready for the battering that was about to come.

'Moira was ready for him,' said John. 'Hook, line and sinker. Speed dating, all right. Did you even have time to buy her a drink?'

'How dare you,' said Murdo.

'What do you mean, "How dare he?"' said Ian. 'You were out that door in a flash. Mind you, you were back in five minutes later.'

'That's about all he's good for these days,' said John.

'Shut up,' said Murdo. 'Who's six feet from the hole here?'

'Aye,' said John. 'It's obviously put a bit of pep in your step, eh?'

Murdo threw a friendly punch at John and told him to get on with it. He was currently twenty feet from the hole. John stepped up, barely looking at the hole, whacking the ball to within about another five feet.

'Well, looks like Romeo's got this hole,' said John.

'Don't be so sure—that's not dead,' said Ian. 'That ball is nowhere near dead!'

'Shut up and putt yours,' said Murdo. 'See if I've got three putts for the hole, maybe even four, by the time you get holed out.'

Murdo stepped back and watched as Ian drained the putt in front of him. *We've had a few specks of rain as well,* thought Murdo. *Not that it would matter much in this course.*

Murdo had been a decent golfer in his day, when he'd worked over on the mainland. He was Barra from birth, but he had worked away from the island for a while and played some rather decent courses. He'd even got down to a single figure handicap. But when he'd come back, it had been after five or six years of not playing, and now it was as much to get out and about as it was to actually try and shoot a decent round.

Murdo stood up, stepped over the ball and set the putt rolling. It looked good; after all, it only had six feet to go, but at the last second, almost unreasonably, it seemed to hop off to the right.

'Not enough pace,' said Ian, teasing him.

'Not enough pace, my arse,' said Murdo. He stepped forward with his putter and flattened down the bump in the green. 'I'll have to have a word with the groundskeeper,' said Murdo.

'You do that,' laughed Ian. 'Come on—next hole; need to keep moving.'

They picked up their golf bags lying beside the green, and wandered over to the third hole. The tee box hung by the edge of the water, the green a little bit further in from it, but there were rocks situated off to the left-hand side. It was Murdo's turn to hit, and he took out his three-iron, teed up his ball, and addressed it.

The wind was just a bit off the left. If he started it that way and cut it back, he should hit the fairly generous fairway.

He drew the club back slowly, head focused on the ball, and as he was about to swing through, he was suddenly interrupted.

'What the hell's that?'

Murdo, in the middle of his downswing, continued, but was clearly disturbed. His hands went through too early. The head of the club came in about a foot behind the ball and an enormous divot was dug up.

Ian burst out laughing for a moment until he saw that John was still pointing. It obviously hadn't been a comedy moment. John had seen something. Something not right.

'What the hell?' said Murdo. 'That stung my hands in the ground. The club's still shaking.'

'What the hell's that?' said John. He dropped his own rescue club and began to walk across the tee, past Murdo and onto the beach. The rocks were not that far away, maybe thirty yards, and Murdo, leaving his club behind, turned to follow him.

'What's the matter?' he asked.

'Are we really doing this?' said Ian. 'That weather's going to come in. If we hang about out here, we'll get a soaking. I'm telling you, we don't want to dally about.'

'Something's there. Something not right,' said John.

Murdo followed him, and then swore, as his foot disappeared into a murky puddle of the sand and water, left behind by the sea.'

'Watch your feet, Ian? There's puddles here everywhere. Little pools from the tide.'

The men were dressed in jeans and jumpers, very different to what Murdo would have worn for a round on the mainland. But here, if it was dry, jeans were the best clothing to wear, keeping you protected from the wind. Murdo had a full set of waterproofs in the bag, because you wouldn't get caught out here in that heavy rain, although none of them had umbrellas. It was usually too windy to bother.

Murdo looked down at his feet, negotiating the puddles, but when he looked up, he saw John was still walking that straight line, and was approaching the figure he'd pointed at. *Was it a figure? What was it?* It was a something, dark against the lighter parts of the rock that were lying on top of it.

'Oh, bloody hell,' said John. He turned and walked away quickly, before bending and vomiting.

'What the blazes is it?' said Murdo. But John was doubled over now, retching out whatever was still left.

'You all right, John?' said Ian. The two men ran over towards their playing partner, and Ian stood beside him, thumping him on the back, helping him get out the last of his sick. Neither one looked at what John had seen but as John began to cough and finally pull himself back together, he stared up into Murdo's eyes.

John's eyes were wet with tears. 'Dear God, Murdo. Dear God.'

Murdo had been a fireman back in the day, when he'd started looking for work. As Ian was an accountant and John a man who worked with computers, Murdo felt it should be his duty to take a good look at whatever was there.

He turned, steeling himself, and slowly walked over. He could see the legs now, probably male. Quickly, he approached what was obviously a body of some sort. And then he recoiled.

Gray flannel trousers. It led up to a belt with a dark black shirt. But as he followed that shirt up, the neck was covered in blood. Murdo took a step back for a moment. The neck had been slashed, probably with some sort of knife, by the looks of it. Blood was on the beach all around. Dark and unrelenting.

He couldn't see any movement from the man. Nothing at all. The eyes were closed while the head had grey hair and faint strands across it. The man was also unshaven, bits of white in his fledgling beard.

'What is it, Murdo?' said a voice from behind him.

'Stay back,' said Murdo. 'Just stay back. Nothing we can do for this one.'

Murdo sucked in the air. Thankfully, it still smelt of the sea. That saltiness, tinged with a little bit of smelly seaweed. It did that occasionally when it got caught up somewhere. Seaweed rotted and left a pungent odour across the beaches. It was only faint, though, due to the wind being reasonable.

Murdo stole forward and then crouched down beside the body. He could feel the bile in his throat wanting to rise. He had seen more horrific sights, and he was fighting not to remember them. It was the child, the child that had been burnt that always got him.

That's why he'd left. That's why he'd decided he couldn't do the fire service anymore. But over the years, he'd put that behind him, locked it away in a cabinet of the mind. But this body in front of him was taking the key out and trying to open it again. Murdo decided he needed to concentrate, have a look around the man, and remember some details for he'd have to phone it in.

Out here in Barra, it wouldn't be a case of the police just popping in from the nearby town. It would take time to get people here. You might get responders from the coastguard or ambulance—whoever, whatever, to maintain the area.

The man's shirt looked funny though. It was almost too inflated, like there was something behind it. Murdo looked around and saw a little washed-up timber, nothing bigger than a small stick. He reached over, picked it up and came back to the shirt. Reaching down with the stick, he pulled the shirt back. Some of the buttons had come off. Maybe the shirt had been forced open. As he pulled it back, he saw a plastic zippy bag.

'Boys,' said Murdo. 'Anybody got the phone on them?'

'I have,' said Ian.

'Make a call. I think we're going to need to keep this place as clean as we can. This doesn't look good.'

'Good,' said the voice behind him. 'I could tell it didn't look good.'

'No, no,' said Murdo. 'Somebody's stuck a book down his shirt.'

'A what?'

'A book down his shirt.' Murdo leaned forward, pulling back a bit more of the shirt, and then continued, until it was as open as it could be, without forcing the remaining buttons to open.

He bent in closely. 'I think it's that book. The one your missus likes. That author—John.'

'McGrubbin?'

'Yeah,' said Murdo. 'It's a book by McGrubbin. I think it says number one.'

'McGrubbin's got a load of different ones. The missus is reading the latest one, but it depends what series it is and stuff.'

'This looks like crime,' said Murdo. 'I think it's a crime book. Cover looks like it's crime.'

'What's the title?' asked John.

What's the bloody title? Why on earth is he asking for the title? thought Murdo. *I've got a man here with a slashed throat and John wants to know what's the title of the book he's holding. Oh well, might keep the mind off the other things.* He peered down.

Two's a Squeeze.

Two's a Squeeze? That's the first in the crime series. Oh, that's old. That's been out for a few years now.'

'It's in a zippy bag. Who carries a book in a zippy bag?'

'We need to get the police here,' said Ian. 'That don't look right.'

'He's got his throat slashed open,' said Murdo. 'Of course, it's not right.'

Murdo stood up and flung the stick away, and walked back to his colleagues.

'What do we do?' asked Ian.

'You phone the police and tell them. Then we stay on the tee box and we make sure nobody else comes near that body,' said Murdo.

'It's going to rain soon.'

'Aye,' said Murdo, 'but we don't do anything else. They'll tell us if they want us to do anything. And one of us will go up and get the waterproofs, some proper coats and that.'

'And a bottle of whisky,' said Ian. 'I'll not stand beside this without a drink.'

'Aye,' said Murdo, passing his eyes back at the unmoving figure on the rocks. He could see a burnt child now. 'You bring the whisky,' he said. 'Decent size bottle, too.'

Chapter 02

Hope lay back on the bed, her red hair splayed on the pillow as she felt the covers being pulled down. She wore a long t-shirt, and her partner John was currently lifting it up, revealing the rather small bump just below her belly. He leaned in, his ear pressing against it.

'Not too hard,' she said. 'Don't hold the water so easily these mornings.'

'Shh, shh,' said John. 'I need to hear.' He turned and spoke to Hope's stomach. 'It's your dad here. What are you up to this morning? Are you still asleep?'

Hope reached down with her hand and tussled John's hair. She laughed. What was he like? It was good though—the beginnings of a family. 'Junior,' as they'd decided to call the bump, was doing okay—unlike Hope. She'd been struggling with morning sickness.

Even in her wilder days, she never felt so bad when being so sick. She remembered when she was younger, drinking alcohol to stupid o'clock in the morning, and suffering for it the next day. But this was different, this was . . .

She grabbed John's head, pushing it to one side.

'Oi!' he said, but her legs were already swinging off the bed.

She stood up and ran, finding the bathroom, kneeling down in front of the toilet, and reaching round with her hand to grab her hair and pull it together. The next minute, all she could focus on was that pool of water in front of her.

An arm went around her shoulder. 'That's it,' said a voice. 'That's it, all gone now.'

He meant well. John really did. He was there to comfort her, but all she wanted to say was 'piss off.' It was bloody awful.

Hope loved being pregnant. She loved the idea that the beginnings of her family were currently residing within her. But she hated this sickness, and quite irrationally, John got the blame for some of that. After all, he had got her pregnant, or at least, whenever she was kneeling down in front of the toilet, that's what raced through her mind.

He, of course, hadn't got her pregnant—they had both got her pregnant, but the inside of a toilet bowl will do that to you.

As she continued to kneel, trying to get rid of the last vestiges of what was coming up, Hope could hear the vibration of her phone.

'Check that for me, please,' she said to John.

'It can wait,' he said.

'No,' she said. 'Check it for me. They won't call. They know I've been suffering a bit. Won't do it unless it's important.'

'Could just be a message from someone. Could just be a text.'

'John, it's vibrating. It's still vibrating. Just get the damn phone for me, please.'

He's overprotective, Hope thought, *which is probably nicer than being under-protective, not giving a toss about me. A lot of the men do this. Just because I'm suddenly pregnant, they step in to make sure I don't overdo anything.*

Doors that never were held open for her before were

suddenly moved aside like she was royalty. Everyone in the station knew, and on the team, it felt like the baby was almost theirs. Part of their family.

'It's Macleod,' said John.

'What's he want?' asked Hope. She thought about getting up to take the call but at the moment she just needed a few more minutes.

'He says it's Barra. Body on Barra. Bad one. Needs you.'

'Bollocks,' spat Hope into the toilet bowl. 'Barra. Inverness to Barra.' She looked at the watch on her wrist. *Flights were going to be a pain. Maybe if they got in the car. When did the ferry go? They could get over if she was quick. They could get to the ferry and then get the other ferries down.*

'Ask him what the sea state's like.'

'What?' said John.

'Just ask him, "What's the sea state like?"'

'He says it's good, says yes.'

'Tell him to ring Perry and Ross. I want to go by ferry and tell him to do it. I'll be in, in'—she looked at her watch again—'in the office within the hour.'

'Are you sure about that?' said John.

Oh, bloody hell, thought Hope. *Don't, just don't.* 'Yes, dear,' she said. 'I'm totally happy about that and that's what I'm doing.'

It took most of the day to journey down to Barra via the sea route, and Macleod had been right—the sea state was okay. They'd had to take the ferry across to Lewis, and driven down to Harris. Then another ferry over from the Sound of Harris down to North Uist and then via Benbecula and South Uist to eventually get their third ferry onto Barra.

They were arriving rather late at night but she was in good company with DC's Perry and Cunningham and DS Ross.

They'd come with two cars because they never knew quite where investigations would go.

Jona and the forensic team had followed with the van. Ross had organised for the coastguard to attend the scene. They'd put a large tent up over the body, preserving it, assisting the police with reinforcements coming in from the Uists. Amazingly, by the time they'd arrived, there were already Press there, being held back by a police cordon.

The golf course was on the west side of the small island of Barra, and being dark, the entire scene was now lit up by generator light. But Hope carried her own torch and was now dressed in an all-weather suit, orange with 'POLICE' on the back. It was thick and warm.

When they'd arrived, Hope had sent Jona off to look at the body first and to make sure she was happy with the scene. Hope advised she'd be along briefly, looking for initial thoughts about what had happened.

'Those who found the body were golfers,' said Hope.

'I've got the names,' said Ross, 'from the local guys. Apparently, they've got them down at the station now making statements.'

'The station?'

'Well, the building.'

'Why don't you and Susan get down there? Take initial thoughts from them. I'll go with Perry, have a look at the scene. Perry can check through the rest around here to make sure we're tight with what we're doing. And I'll talk over with Jona, see if we can work out who this is.'

'Local sergeant said to me he had no idea,' said Ross. 'Didn't think the man was local. Certainly, none of the locals have recognised anyone missing or new about.'

'How many people have got close?' asked Hope.

'Well, there was the initial three. That's what the officer said. But a couple of others popped over for a look before they could set the scene up properly. Once the coastguard was out, they could manage the place better. They're locals of course too, and they had a look and didn't recognise him.'

'Very good,' said Hope. She turned to Perry. 'How are we doing for accommodation for the night?'

'I've got you booked in a small hotel. I'm trying to see if there's a house or anything we can rent.'

'Okay,' said Hope. She took a walk around the perimeter, talking to a few of the local officers, and then heard a shout from Jona advising she was ready. Hope was led by Jona, on a circuitous route round towards the scene. Hope didn't get too close up, but the lights from the generator showed a gruesome vista.

'He's died here,' said Jona, 'by being slashed across the throat. Proper knife. I mean, it's cut right through. The man had no chance. He's probably been held while doing it, given the precision of the cut. You'd have thought he would be struggling. But I'll have a look and see if he was drugged or whatever. Possibly held from behind. Not seeing any footprints at the moment, but we'll have a look. We'll have a search for everything. There's a book with the body. I'll get that out, up to the van, and have a look at it. But it's very bizarre.'

'A book with the body?' said Hope. 'What do you mean?'

'There's a book inside a zippy bag that's been stuffed inside the shirt. Probably after death. I'm not sure. Some of the shirt buttons are ripped to make room for the book. I think it's a fairly tight shirt. The man himself, as you can see, is probably in his seventies or beyond. No one seems to know who he is, but the photographs are done. We'll put them up onto the case cloud. See if anyone can recognise him, run facial recognition, all the usual stuff. Take fingerprints and that.'

'He died here, though?' said Hope.

'Yes, he died here,' said Jona.

'So, you've had to have come down the golf course, or across these fields, to get down here. Somebody would have had to have carried him in, or led him in.'

'If he came from the land,' said Jona. 'You could come from the sea. At least I think you could. Certainly, you could run a small tender onto this beach.'

'But why? Why would you come all the way out here to slash someone's throat? It makes little sense,' said Hope.

'Maybe you wouldn't be seen,' said Jona.

'It's beside a golf course. How do you know somebody will not be golfing? How do you know you're clear? Why here? Where are we anyway?'

'It seems bizarre,' said Jona. 'Why out to the Isle of Barra? Not a local man.'

'How long are you going to be with the book?' asked Hope.

'Just finishing my notes. Then I'll take it out and take it up. I'll see you in about fifteen minutes.'

Hope nodded and walked back up towards where the car was parked. She placed a call down to Ross and he messaged back, saying he was in the middle of the interviews. She caught up with Perry, who seemed quite happy with the security of the situation. He said he chased a few Press people off for the night, advising that Hope would make a statement in the morning.

After checking in with Macleod and giving some brief details about what was going on, Hope was called over by Jona into the forensics wagon. Inside, dressed in her full gear, Jona undid the zippy bag and took out the book that had been lying inside the shirt of the body.

'I recognise that one.'

'You what?' blurted Jona.

'I recognise that one. *Two's a Squeeze.*'

'You've got me,' said Jona.

'K.F. McGrubbin. I read those. Bit far-fetched, really. Crime ones, though. Read them when I was out on a beach somewhere. I think it might have been Greece, lying under the sun all day. I mean, far-fetched, not like what I do. But, you know, entertaining read. She's made it big now, McGrubbin. Lots of books. A few different genres, as well.'

Jona took the book and slowly opened the pages. One by one, she went through it, but there was nothing inside. No annotations, no bookmarks, nothing.

'This is pristine.'

'I wonder if we can find out where it was sold. There's no sticker on these things nowadays, is there?'

'No,' said Jona. 'All barcode scanned.'

'She sells well, though, McGrubbin. Would be a hiding to nothing. What would it prove? Who's going to remember who bought a McGrubbin book? Or when it was bought? Even if you tag that down, how are you going to explain it being here?'

Hope went to turn away, and then stopped. 'Why, though?' she said. 'Why on earth would you put this book here? *Two's a Squeeze.*" We don't even have two people here.'

'Do you remember the book?'

'No,' said Hope. 'Not in detail. Something to do with somebody getting murdered. Something to do with the body.

I can't remember.'

'Seems strange,' said Jona. 'Why leave a book with a body and in a zippy bag? It's not like our victim was carrying it.'

'Well, the zippy bag's to make sure it's maintained, isn't it?' said Hope. 'You'll struggle here without that. The weather, everything else. How do you know when the body's going to get spotted?'

Hope stopped for a moment, thinking. She put her hand out and grabbed the table.

'You okay?' asked Jona.

'Long day.'

'You still having the morning sickness?'

'Full on,' said Hope. 'Thought it would start to go away soon.'

'Some women have it all the way through,' said Jona, and saw Hope's look. 'Sorry, I should have said something a bit more optimistic there.'

'You probably should,' said Hope.

Jona pulled out a chair, and Hope sat down.

'Carried out a murder by the golf club. Why? You're remote, but you're also somewhere that somebody at some point will see it. Do you think the tides could have pulled that body back out?'

Jona expanded the map function on one of her tablets. She started going through charts of the sea.

'Looking at where the tide lines are, no. We can corroborate that with the coastguard here, but I don't think that body would have got shifted out much, if at all. It's up on the rock as well. High likelihood that the body would stay there.'

'So somebody wanted us to find it, or somebody to find it. Somebody left a book,' said Hope.

'What are you thinking?' asked Jona.

'If somebody gets slashed in the throat, or somebody gets murdered, often,' said Hope, 'that's it. It's a rash act. But this person has been brought to a remote place, but yet somewhere where a body will be found and can't be moved by the elements. And has a golf course beside it, which people are going to play on from time to time; therefore, meaning that the body will be seen. They've also left a book. The book's to tell us something. The body has to be found. And he's killed here. Not killed before and dumped. Would have been much quicker, much easier.'

'And?' said Jona.

'Somebody's trying to send a message. Somebody's making a statement,' said Hope. 'Trouble is that when you make statements like this, you don't usually just make one.'

Chapter 03

There was thunder. Loud thunder. But that wasn't bothering Hope. After all, there was so much else to get on with. She looked at the sword in her hand, glared down at the leather boots on her feet, the straps of leather that ran up her legs. She had a loincloth on, as well as a rough shirt. Her hair was tied back with leather strapping.

Across her back was a papoose holding the child. She looked at the creatures coming for them. Again, the thunder hammered—nothing would take this babe from her, nothing!

Hope's eyes flicked open. *Thump* came a rap on the door. Hope flung back the covers, spun out with her legs and looked around, grabbing her dressing gown and putting it on. She half-stumbled over to the door.

'Who is it?' she said.

'Sorry, boss, it's Perry. It's getting to eight o'clock. You said you were going to do the press conference at half eight. I thought I should make sure you're awake.'

Hope reached down and opened up the door. She pulled it back and waved Perry in.

'Stall it,' she said to Perry.

He looked a little awkward with Hope in her dressing gown

and he tried to look the other way.

'Give them some excuse—new information, called in by somebody, you know the usual, Perry. And I'll do it at nine, okay? I just need to—'

Hope shoved Perry out of the way and tore off to the ensuite bathroom. She threw up the toilet lid, got down on her knees, then felt her stomach erupting. Hope felt her hair being lifted and held behind her. She didn't resist, but continued until she had finished.

'If you're okay, I'll just get out,' said Perry. 'You looked like you were having—'

'It's fine, Perry,' said Hope, spitting into the bowl ahead of her. 'Can you help me up?'

Perry held out a hand, helped Hope up, and then turned and wet a flannel for her, offering it to her to wipe her mouth. By the time she'd stepped back into her bedroom, she'd heard the toilet flush, and the flannel was being taken back off her to be rinsed. He really was quite domesticated.

'Should I get Susan to come?' said Perry.

'I should be all right,' said Hope. 'This just happens, Perry. You know, it's just morning sickness.'

'It looks pretty rough,' he said.

'Apparently it's all part of pregnancy, at least for some of us.'

'I wouldn't know,' said Perry. 'I'll tell them half nine. You should have a proper breakfast. You need to take care. Need to—'

'Perry,' said Hope suddenly. 'What you did was very kind, but this thing of telling me what I should do, that won't work. It doesn't work for John. It's certainly not going to work for my constable.'

'Sorry. You just looked like you needed help.'

'And I did,' said Hope. 'And you have. But if I need more than that, I'll tell you, and I'll decide when and where I'm doing stuff. Nine o'clock. Organise them, yes?'

'Okay,' said Perry. He turned to go to the door, and Hope tapped him on the shoulder.

'Sorry,' she said. 'It's a bit much, and I'm snippy, and I get annoyed with people telling me what I should do. You're only trying to help, and you have helped. I can see why Susan's fond of you.'

Perry seemed to smile for a minute, then he simply nodded and went to leave the room, but before he did, he stopped and turned. 'The book you found—what was the title again?'

'*Two's a Squeeze*,' said Hope. 'K.F. McGrubbin. Have you read it?'

'Not yet,' said Perry, and with that, he left the room.

Hope had a quick shower and then dressed. Dressing was becoming more of a faff than usual. She was having to watch what she wore.

Hope had always liked her jeans, but with the developing bump, it wasn't always a good option. However, they made pregnancy jeans, with more elasticity around the front. She wasn't at a stage now where she felt encumbered, but that would come, too. She really needed to sit and plan with Macleod when she was stopping, when she was going to have her time off and talk to John about afterwards.

When will I come back? Macleod had said it was not a problem. She'd take her full maternity. She'd work whenever she could, but this child was the most important thing she was going to be doing in the next year. Not the case.

Hope made her way down and had a simple breakfast before coming back up to her room and placing a call through to

Macleod.

'Morning. How's my best ray of sunshine today?' asked Macleod. This was something else he was starting to do. It was his way of not asking after her directly, but kind of making a joke about it. But he was checking up on her. Everyone was making sure she was okay. He was just a little more subtle.

'I'm fine,' she said. 'Absolutely fine. Now the case.'

'Yes, the case,' said Macleod. 'I've had a look at the photograph you sent up.'

'Gruesome, isn't it?' said Hope. 'Also doesn't bode well. Somebody's sending a message.'

'McGrubbin book. Never read it,' said Macleod. *Two's a Squeeze.'*

'I have,' said Hope. 'Remember little about it. I was sunsoaked on a Greek beach back then. It's been a while, too. Over ten years at least, if not more.'

'Did you enjoy it?' asked Macleod.

'I think so. Passed the time, whatever it was. I think it's important, though,' said Hope. 'I just have no idea why.'

'The other thing that's important,' said Macleod, 'is I think I recognise the face.'

'You know who he is?'

'No, I said I recognise the face,' said Macleod. 'One of those faces which has passed me by at some point. I don't know where.'

'Is it your social life? Work?'

'Work,' said Macleod. 'Had little social life down in Glasgow. Don't have that much of a social life up here either.'

'Now that's a lie,' said Hope. 'You think it's Glasgow?'

'Well, you don't recognise him, do you? He's not from work up here, as none of the team recognise him. We all work up here. Something tells me it's Glasgow, where I used to work. But I didn't work with him, not directly.'

'You want me to bump it down, then, to see if anybody—'

'No,' said Macleod.

Hope found that a little strange. 'Any particular reason?' asked Hope.

'Let's not alert people.'

'Alert who?' asked Hope.

'Send Perry.' Macleod went silent, not answering her question.

'Why Perry?' asked Hope.

'Used to work with me down in Glasgow. Knows the terrain. Knows the people.'

'Do you think I should get him to take a closer look, see if he remembers?'

'If Perry remembered that face in any vague sense or form, he'd have told you by now,' said Macleod. 'But he probably would have rung me up as well to tell me if he knew who it was. Or he'd have asked me to look if he remembered him from his face.'

'But that's why we should send the image down,' said Hope. 'Plenty of people down there were working right back to when you started. The dead man appears in his, what, seventies? Maybe they'll recognise him. Anyone aged from what, thirty to fifty, sixty even, may remember.'

'It's a dead body, and it's an older face than I probably would have seen,' said Macleod. 'But I know the face from somewhere.'

'And that's why I'm saying canvass them down there. Let's put it wide,' said Hope.

'No,' said Macleod. 'Send Perry. Tell him to be quiet about

it. Subtle. Don't cause a stir.'

'Why?' asked Hope.

Macleod went silent for a moment.

'Do you not think that this could be one of many, one of more to come? The book and that?' said Hope.

'Yes. That's why I don't want you to put it out too quickly,' said Macleod.

'I don't follow,' said Hope.

'If this is potentially one of ours, maybe it's an in-station thing. Maybe it's somebody within the police network that's done it.'

'That's a bit of a stretch,' said Hope.

'Till we know what we're dealing with, let's not go too wide on this. This isn't a straightforward murder—this is, as you said, saying something. So, let's just keep it under our hats, go about it easily, smoothly, under the radar. Perry will do that—he's good like that. He can read the terrain, and if he thinks he's got it in front of somebody who's hiding something, he'll know.'

'Do that initially,' said Hope, 'but if we don't get anywhere, I want to put it wide and not too long after.'

'Thanks,' said Macleod, 'what else are you up to?'

'Do the press conference and then we'll try to see if the locals know anything.'

'Did anything come from those people who had seen the body? Your golfers?'

'No, we interviewed them last night and they know nothing about him. I'm not sure how he got there yet,' said Hope. 'So we're going to have a look around all the local hostelries, anywhere that's put people up, canvas for friends, family staying. But Jona said an interesting thing. She said that they didn't have to come from the land. They could have brought him from the sea.'

'Still don't get why they're there,' said Macleod. 'Why that place? What's with the book? Why slash a neck, there? Why bring him alive? How's Jona doing anyway?'

'She's been up all night. I'll catch her again this morning. But she's made herself a makeshift lab. Eventually, she'll take the body back up to Stornoway. And then ship it over to Inverness. I think we could be here for two or three days at least, if not longer. Certainly, Jona will want to get the entire area covered. See if we can dig out any footprints. But with the tide coming in, it's liable to have washed away most of the footprints.'

'So the body could have disappeared back out?'

'No, where the tide comes up, he was left on rocks. Those rocks are never soaked. The idea that the body would drift off would have been highly unlikely. It was meant to be found,' said Hope.

'I'll let you get on,' said Macleod. 'Keep in touch. I'm here if you need me. Take care of yourself.'

Hope thanked him and closed down the call. 'Take care of yourself.' There it was again. Macleod was making sure she was looking after herself, making sure that she was on top of her pregnancy. She got sick of it. She was pregnant, not ill.

And then she felt it. Hope stumbled through to the bathroom again. It wasn't as bad this time, but it took her a few minutes to sort herself out before marching down for the press conference. It was a routine affair. Standard information. Investigations are ongoing. Anyone with information, please contact.

Afterwards, she spoke with Ross. He was getting a canvas organised to go round everyone on the island to see if anyone knew the man, photographs at the ready. But the place was abuzz with the talk of it. Not surprising. It was a brutal murder. Here in the back of, well, beyond, as they would say in Glasgow. The islands were far out for Scotland, weren't they?

Hope met with Jona again and she advised Hope that there was no ID on the man. That was the thing as well. If you were making a statement, wouldn't you have left ID in the man's clothes? Why wouldn't he have had ID? Most people carried ID on them. You'd have taken it off him. But why? Why would you take it off him if you were sending a message, whatever that message was.

Jona had done fingerprints and was sending them off to see if she could get a match. She was checking his DNA too for a match. She said it would take time, though. And that's what bothered Hope. Whenever you had a killing like this and you thought another one was coming, the one thing you didn't have was time. And worse than that, you didn't know how much time you did or didn't have.

Maybe, just maybe, the local trawl would come up with something.

Chapter 04

Alan Ross stood on the streets of Castlebay, looking at the other officers around him, stopping people. They were holding up pictures of the deceased man, cleaned up from the image that had first presented itself to the golfers. The small town was awash with rumour and ideas about who the man was, except nothing concrete.

Nobody knew him. Nobody had seen him. This was the funny part of the trawl, though. You were hoping to get lucky, to hit upon somebody who had seen something. But everywhere they turned, nothing was coming back.

'How are you getting on?' Ross asked Susan, coming across Cunningham.

'Dead end so far from everyone. It's like he hasn't been here at all.'

'Might be the case,' said Ross. 'You never know. He's certainly not local. Small communities like this, they know everyone. Anyone that's been living here, even relatives who visit. Somebody usually knows someone. He'll be an outsider, somebody from elsewhere.'

'When are you wanting to go for the ferry?' Ross had plans to interview the ferry staff on the vessel that served Barra.

'It'll be here in a minute. They said they're going to stop for an extra half hour. We can run on and look round the crew. See if any of them know our man.'

'Very good. We'll do the port staff at the same time,' said Susan. 'Then up to the airport.'

'Leave the other officers here. We'll do the travel points,' said Ross.

'Let's hope it brings up something,' said Susan.

'Yes, there's nowhere else to go at the moment. Although, Perry's disappearing off. He's going down to Glasgow. Apparently, the big boss thinks he might have known the face, but from way back.'

'It's not like him,' said Susan. 'He wouldn't interfere like that unless he's pretty sure.'

'I don't know,' said Ross. 'This is just that time in the investigation. Get a start, get a foothold in somewhere. It'll come. Anyway, come on, let's head off down to the port.'

As they walked, Susan was struck by a woman with red hair and sunglasses on. She didn't think it was sunny enough. Nowadays, people wore them as a fashion accessory as much as anything else, so she thought little of it. Except that the woman looked toned, in good shape, and Susan rather liked the boots she was wearing.

When the ferry docked, Ross and Susan Cunningham were taken on board and introduced quickly to the captain. He assembled his crew all together in one room, where Ross gave them a briefing on what had happened.

He held up and distributed photographs of the man, asking if anyone remembered him travelling with the boat. They were still on their two-week rotation, almost nearing the end, so the likelihood that this crew would have seen him if he'd come in by ferry was reasonably high. He also didn't seem to have been among the populace for very long.

'And we're absolutely sure?' said Ross. 'Not even a hint?'

'I don't know what else to say,' said the captain. 'Nobody remembers him.' He looked down towards his hospitality crew, those who would have served in the canteen and in the small cafe bar of the ferry. They were all shaking their heads.

'That's fair enough,' said Ross. 'It was worth a shot. Thanks for your help.'

They shook hands with the captain, and soon Susan and Ross entered the small terminal for the ferry. There were only a couple of staff there, and speaking to them, the officers found only shaking heads there, too.

'You clocked me earlier on up in the town,' said one man. 'Said to them, no one I recognise. It's bizarre though, isn't it? Brutal. And what's that book with him, anyway? Somebody told me it was the *Kama Sutra*.'

'I'm afraid that's a rumour,' said Ross. 'It'd be a more entertaining case if it was.'

Ross laughed, but when he turned away from the man, he was shaking his head almost imperceptibly. *How rumours spread. 'The Kama Sutra.' How do you go from 'Two's a Squeeze' to the 'Kama Sutra'?* No, Ross would not try to put those two together.

'I think it's time to head up to the airport,' she said to Susan.

'Okay,' she said. 'Just a minute.'

Ross watched as Susan stood just outside the terminal, peering across the car park. She then gave a nod and began walking towards the car. After a bit, she said to Ross, 'Let's go this way.'

'But the car's up here,' he said.

'I know, but I think we should take a little circuit.'

'Constable,' said Ross, 'we're not here to enjoy the scenery, we're here to—'

'Something's bothering me. For that reason, indulge me, please. Let's take a wee walk.'

The two strode along, and Ross was impressed at Susan Cunningham's prosthetic leg. It was almost as if she hadn't lost the other one. He knew it was different when she'd been running full tilt but she was coping now—almost come to embrace the way she was.

'I think someone's following us,' Susan said quickly, interrupting Ross's thoughts.

'Really?' said Ross.

'She had a skirt on this time. Long one, though. Could have covered the jeans that she had on previously.'

'You're not just getting a little paranoid after your trip to Italy?'

Susan looked up at him, shaking her head. 'No, I'm not, Sergeant. I think this person might be keeping tabs on us. Could be a journalist.'

They continued their circuitous route and came back to the car park, but Susan couldn't see the woman anywhere.

'Are you happy now? Can we go to the airport?' said Ross. Susan nodded. The trip up to the airport wasn't long, and soon they were talking to the security staff and those that manned the information point.

It took a while to go through each of them, before talking to those who were ground crew for the airline. As a last resort, they also took a trip to the tower to speak to the flight information service officers and any ancillary staff that worked there. That was a long shot. After all, those who worked in the control tower had only seen the aircraft from a distance.

It was with regret that Ross ended up shaking hands with the airport supervisor and then heading back towards the car. But once again, Susan Cunningham stopped him.

'There's an aircraft just landing there. Did you see that?' she said.

'Yes,' said Ross. 'Got busier in the terminal.'

'It did, didn't it?' said Susan. 'Did you see her?'

'Did I see who?'

'Red-headed woman.'

'No,' said Ross. 'I was kind of busy seeing if anybody recognised the face on this photograph. That's what we're here for.'

'Something's not right. Somebody was watching us. I'm sure of it.'

'Why?' asked Ross. 'Why would someone be watching us? If it's the press, at some point they're going to stop us and say, "Can I get your take on this?" Or we'll be able to phone back and see if anybody's been pestering them. In fact, that's an idea. Phone the port. See if anybody with red hair has been in and pestered them.'

The look on Ross's face told Susan she was doing the action and so she didn't hesitate and called back down to the ferry port. There had been nobody there. No one had spoken to them. Susan got into the car with Ross. But as the car passed out of the car park, Susan thought she saw the red hair again.

'What?' said Ross.

'That car. I'm sure there was someone in that car.'

'Let me guess,' said Ross. 'With red hair?'

'Yes. With red hair.'

'Did you catch the number plate?' asked Ross.

'No,' said Susan. 'Turned too quickly. Black car, though.

Hatchback.'

'Okay then. We'll see if there was a black hatchback.'

They drove back into town to catch up with the officers who were doing the street trawl. Parking up, they made their way along to find each of them in turn at the various spots they'd set up to hand out the leaflets. As they approached one, Susan grabbed Ross.

'That car—that's a black car.'

'Yes, and it's a hatchback,' said Ross.

'It's the right design. It was a car like that,' she said.

Ross picked up his phone and called in to the station. He asked for a check on the number plate. He got the owner's name and address back. They lived here in Barra.

'Come on, let's talk to one of the local officers.'

Ross knew one of the constables lived in Barra, so Ross went directly to him, asking if he knew the name and address of the person who the car belonged to.

'Oh yes,' he said. 'Andrea, I know her well.'

'What kind of hair does she have?' asked Ross.

'She's a blonde. Why?'

'I thought there might have been a redhead driving that car.'

'Well, their daughter's got black hair, son's black, husband's nearly bald. There's nobody in that family with red hair.'

Ross gives Susan a look and then turned back to the constable. 'Any luck with the photographs?'

'I'll tell you now . . . nobody here has seen this man. No one's come forward. People would, you know. People would; this is, this is shocking. We don't get this sort of thing. You might get the odd theft. You might get somebody who's drunk to fall off a pier, or something. An accident, or a fist fight, two drunken fools. You don't get someone with their throat slashed, left on a beach.'

'You don't get that very often in Inverness either,' said Ross, 'but I take your point.'

He turned, but Susan Cunningham was no longer beside him. He saw her disappearing round a corner. Ross, after excusing himself from the officer, quickly strode down the street.

He then glanced up at the street Susan had turned into and saw her disappearing into another one. After another two streets, Ross phoned Susan Cunningham.

'Susan,' she said.

'Where are you going?' asked Ross. 'Can you just tell me what you're doing?'

'I think there's definitely someone watching us. I've lost her now, though. Red hair, same boots. I'm sure it was.'

'But she hasn't come for you and she's watching us walking around to the ferry and the airport. It'll be a journalist at worst,' said Ross. 'Don't worry about it. Come on; we've got work to do.'

'I'll catch you up.'

Ross waited while Susan retraced her steps before joining him. As he walked along the street, he said to her, 'Do funny things, incidents. You were really under the cosh out in Italy, from what I've heard. Macleod doesn't tell the entire story, but he's told enough of it. In some ways, you were lucky to get out alive, but you got deceived. Encounters with the more clandestine people starts putting ideas in your head that they're there all the time.'

'Is this your way of explaining to me I've got an overactive imagination?' asked Susan. 'Because you can just tell me. I didn't come back from Italy deluded or overly traumatised.

And I know these people and how they operate more now. This woman was furtive today.'

'I'm telling you, it's probably just a journalist. Looking to catch out little bits of information. Looking to see who we're talking to and then to catch us out when we say something. I wouldn't worry about it. The boss will not like you worrying about it.'

'Okay,' said Susan. 'I won't. But if I see her, I'm going to tap this woman on the shoulder and find out who she is. And if she's a journalist, I'm going to read the riot act with her.'

'No, you won't,' said Ross. 'What you will do is get her name and bring it to me. And I'll deal with it if the press is snooping too closely. But they have a right to have a look. They're not breaking the law.'

'I never said she was breaking the law,' said Susan. 'But what she is doing is impeding the investigation if she's peering in on us. More than that, maybe she's somebody else. Because we really know nothing about the case yet. We don't know about this person. We don't—'

'No, we don't,' said Ross. 'But that doesn't mean we open ourselves up to all suspicions, okay? You've clocked someone; you've tried to corner them. You haven't been able to get a hold of them. If it happens again and you're able to get them, then great. We'll deal with it when we catch them. Until then, don't bother. Let's just get on with what we're meant to do. Okay?'

'Okay,' said Susan.

'By the way, I wouldn't even notice anymore.'

'Notice what?' asked Susan.

'Your leg. It's very natural when you walk.'

'It is natural. But I notice,' she said. 'I notice it every day. I still don't wear a skirt.'

'Maybe you should,' said Ross. 'Maybe you should.'

He walked on, and knowing Ross for the person he was, she knew it was a genuine comment. Nothing to do with how Susan looked. But she stopped for a moment.

Maybe the car got moved. Maybe it was stolen and then put back. Couldn't be that easy to move quietly around Barra, could it? She wondered how Perry would have taken her story. Would he have backed her more? Ross just seemed to reject it.

Ross wasn't a field person, was he? He liked his computers. He liked to be knee-deep in paperwork. Susan enjoyed being out and about. And she knew when something was wrong.

Chapter 05

D C Warren Perry walked out of the Glasgow airport terminal and picked up a hire car. The trip over from Barra on the small Twin Otter plane had been bumpy. Perry wasn't the greatest of flyers, but he was armed with a picture of a man, and a determination to find out who he was.

On the way over, he'd been reading, trying to take his mind off the shaking of the plane. He didn't like the word 'turbulence.' That sounded like things were in a spiral. Shaking was better. That way, you thought it was just a little bit of instability, not some sort of frantic spinning around. Turbulent waters were always frantic, weren't they?

Happily installed in a hire car, Perry negotiated the Glasgow traffic, relying on the years he'd spent down here, before arriving at his old station. He'd worked with Macleod for a short while and hadn't been back since his move up to Inverness. It had lots of memories, good and bad, and some were very indifferent. Perry couldn't say he was delighted to see the place again.

He was enjoying where he was now. It was a breath of fresh air, a different team, a different way of working. He was also feeling good about himself up in Inverness. Yes, he'd had a rough time with Susan Cunningham, but now they seemed to be getting back to being friends. Maybe one day they could be a lot more.

He could only do his best. He shouldn't expect so much, though. After all, she was a younger woman. Maybe at some point she'd want a husband, go off and have a family. Now he didn't look like the family man. He'd got to that age where people thought there was something wrong with you if you didn't have a family. That was unfair. There was nothing wrong with Perry. He'd just never met the right person. Or had the desire to have a family. Nothing wrong with that.

He parked in the station car park and marched into the offices that he had known so well. He paid a quick visit to the desk sergeant, just letting him know he was in the station and that he was going around asking about the photograph.

The desk sergeant was a new one, a man he didn't know. He eyed Perry with some suspicion until Perry withdrew his warrant card and mentioned it was on instruction from DCI Macleod. And it had been. Hope had said that. Macleod wanted him to do this. She hadn't been that bothered about it and would rather have just sent the picture on its own.

Perry made his way around the station, stopping different people and asking, but he didn't feel very welcome. Most ignored him. Especially when they realised he was with Macleod. Of course, quite a few would have known that. They knew Perry. And Perry had gone north. Perry had left them.

In the same way that Macleod had gone north. Maybe it was just the fame bit. Not Perry's, but Macleod's. But Perry wasn't sure where the antagonism was coming from. He noticed that there were some who were just simply indifferent. That was one thing about Perry. He could read you like a book. He could tell if you were annoyed with him or if you just were busy.

Or, if indeed, you were hiding something. Though he didn't find anybody hiding something here, he didn't seem to find any friends. Having spent a good four hours at the station and getting nowhere, Perry decided he needed to try another tack.

What about people who worked at the station but who were no longer there? Here, he had a thought. There was a retired inspector he'd worked under before he'd worked with Macleod. That man would have known everybody in the station. Given that the photograph he was holding looked like a seventy or eighty-year-old, the era would have been his.

Perry returned to his car in the car park, and drove through the Glasgow streets until he got to Rutherglen, a semi-affluent part of Glasgow. He parked up on a sweeping hill and looked at the tall building in front of him. Approaching the large front door, he saw the different labels for the flats. The flat at the top was the one he wanted—Inspector Campbell.

The building was the typical almost orange-coloured tenement and the stone steps inside were as depressing as Perry always found them. The door at the top was also plain. When he rang the bell, it took several minutes for the door to be opened, but when it was, a rather dapper man in his eighties suddenly took on a glint in his eye.

'Warren!' he said. 'My lad, if it isn't Perry himself. You were a darn youngster when you came in. Look at you now. Fat as ever.'

'I'm not fat, just well built,' said Perry with a convivial smile. It had been good working in his team. The banter was something else, and Perry did miss it. It could be caustic, full on, but Perry was equal to it and enjoyed it.

'How can I help you?' said former Inspector Campbell.

'Do you mind if I come in, sir?' asked Perry. The man had always been 'sir.' This was long before the days of first names were being used.

'Of course; you'll be wanting a drink, will you? I could do a coffee for you, if you want.'

Perry thanked the man, and soon was sitting in an armchair opposite another one inside the flat. The inspector sat with a tumbler of whisky and what looked like a double measure, while Perry sat with a cup of coffee.

'How can I help you?'

'Here,' said Perry, reaching over, showing the man a picture of the deceased in Barra.

'Well, looking at those eyes and that face, I take it this man's dead.'

'That's the cleaned-up version, but yes,' said Perry.

'And you want me to do what?'

'To see if you can identify him,' said Perry. 'My new boss, DCI Macleod, he seems to think he remembers him from his days in Glasgow.'

Campbell looked at the picture, studying it for a minute or two. He then reached over and grabbed a pair of glasses, squinting at the picture continually. And then he turned to Perry.

'Macleod's right; he will remember him, but he wasn't on Macleod's team. I don't think so.'

'Who is he?'

'That is Desmond Barraclough. Worked in forensics, as much as they were forensics in those days.'

'Desmond Barraclough? I don't remember him,' said Perry.

'Well, you won't. Before your time. Before that little kid came through those doors. You've got chubby, Warren.'

'You told me I was chubby then and you've called me chubby until you retired. I knew it was you when you opened the door and told me I was looking fat.'

'I didn't say you were looking fat,' said Campbell with a laugh. Then he stopped again.

'Desmond Barraclough was in his fifties, working in forensics when I remember him. Oh, it's a good thirty years ago. Something like that. He left,' said Campbell. 'Can't quite remember the reason. Medical. Something like that. Didn't get sacked, didn't get booted on, didn't get moved somewhere else. It was something medical, if I remember right. Campbell? Quietish sort of bloke. Few rumours about him.'

'Rumours about him? How do you mean?' asked Perry.

'Well, back in those days you weren't, well, you know how it's gone these days. You can be anything you want, can't you? Couldn't back then. They said he was a shirt-lifter.'

Perry almost winced at the expression. An old one for a homosexual. A nasty one at that.

'Was he?' asked Perry.

'I don't know,' Campbell said. 'People said a lot of things, at times. Don't know where they got it from. I didn't work closely with the man. Dealt with him a couple of times in the forensics capacity. Professional enough. Don't know what he did, where he went. But it's him, all right. That's Desmond Barraclough. Now, why are you showing me? What's happened to him?'

'Had his throat slashed. Out on Barra.'

'Who did that then?' asked Campbell.

'That's the thing. Might have seen it on the news. Somebody pitched up with him. Cut his throat out on the beach and left him there; left him with a book, tucked inside his shirt.'

'A book?'

'Yes,' said Perry. 'I'm reading the book at the moment, *Two's a Squeeze*, written by McGrubbin.'

'That's that crime crap, isn't it?' said the man. 'That came out a while back, too.'

'I'm reading it at the moment,' said Perry, 'but it was left, no markings in the book, nothing else.'

'You sure he just didn't have it on him?'

'It was in a zippy bag,' said Perry. He looked across at Campbell, who shook his head, turned, and took a large slug of his whisky.

'Well, yep, those days are far behind me. I'm afraid I'll leave you with that one. I can't tell you anything further, really. That's about as much as I remember. Still, good to see you again. Even if it's only to remind myself how slim I look.'

Perry laughed at the man and shook his hand before leaving. He returned to the Glasgow station. Perry found a terminal and dug into the records as best he could. Desmond Barraclough was indeed listed and was also noted as having retired medically. The medical issue was unclear. So, Perry walked along to an HR department, and to one in particular.

He rapped on the door and opened it to see a woman sitting behind a desk. She was in her late forties, long brown hair running down the side of her face in waves.

She didn't look up from her computer, instead putting up a hand and asking the person at the door to wait.

'You always told me to wait. I waited so long I cleared off,' said Perry.

'Oh, look what the cat's dragged in,' said the woman suddenly. She stood up, walked out from behind the desk, and came over to Perry. He put out his hand.

'Tanya,' he said, going to shake her hand.

She stepped forward and hugged him before kissing him on the cheek. 'A handshake? Do I want a mere handshake from you?' she said, and hugged him again.

'Good to see you,' he said. 'You're still looking—'

'Hot. That's the word you want to use, isn't it?' she said. 'You want to use the word hot. Of course, I still look hot.' She laughed.

'And how's he?' asked Perry.

'He isn't. He's gone.'

'I'm sorry,' said Perry.

'I'm not,' Tanya said. 'He was an arsehole. You were right. Always right, Perry. You could always read people.'

'Well, I couldn't read you well enough,' he said.

'There's always time though, isn't there?' said Tanya. 'Why are you here? Sweep me off my feet? I hope so.' Perry turned and closed the door behind him. 'Ah,' said Tanya. 'Work. And I thought you'd come all this way just for me.'

Perry went to speak but was a little flummoxed. If he'd ever known, he might have come all the way down. Tanya and he had been good friends. Very close friends, but never quite got beyond that, though Perry had wanted to. He was sure Tanya had wanted to, as well. But through various experiences, she'd ended up marrying a sergeant who Perry had told her, right before she married him, was an arsehole. He'd been blunt.

In fact, he'd been very blunt. Told her it would ruin her. Told her she wouldn't enjoy it. That the man would sleep around despite having the best body in his own bed. Perry had said too much. But she'd gone ahead and married him. And now she was saying he was right.

'I was saying why have you come down?'

Perry started back to the present. 'We found a body in Barra with a slashed throat.'

'Sorry,' said Tanya. 'I made you nervous, didn't I? We can keep it business if you want.'

Perry wasn't quite sure what he wanted. But he'd keep it business for the minute, anyway.

'Desmond Barrington. Sorry, Barraclough. He used to work here. Forensics or whatever it was called back in the day. Got retired medically. I'm trying to find out why. What the medical reason was.'

'You say you found him? Dead?'

'Yes,' said Perry. 'Throat slashed in Barra. I've come down here with the photograph asking if people recognised him, but nobody seemed to. I found an old inspector that did. He's convinced it's Barraclough. Says he was medically retired, which I've confirmed, but I can't, for the life of me, get in to find out what the condition was because—'

'It's a medical record, isn't it, Perry? Of course you can't get it.'

'I could do with it, though.'

'Why don't you find out who's going to sign off your sheet of paper, to say I can find it for you?'

'You need to do this one on the quiet,' said Perry.

'Why?' asked Tanya.

'Been told to. Told to by the big boss?'

'Macleod? You always had something for him, didn't you? Always liked him. Mind you—he always liked you, too.'

'He wants the information. If I highlight I'm going after it, we can't operate how we want to. A bit in the shadows.'

Tanya leaned forward and ran a hand up the inside of Perry's jacket, pulling him close to her. 'Always thought of you as a spy. Got the brains for it.'

'But not the body,' said Perry.

'That's the thing about you blokes, isn't it? It's all body. And I thought you liked me for my mind.'

'I always did. You're the only one I could talk to. The only one who understood. The only one who—'

'We missed it, didn't we?' she said. 'Missed that point.' She reached up and kissed him on the cheek. 'I'll get you what you want, Perry. Not a problem.'

Tanya disappeared back to her computer. And after a moment or two, she turned round and said, 'Medical retirement with a bad back. All looks very legit. Nothing looks out of order with it. Sorry. If you were looking for something a bit more dramatic.'

'It is what it is,' said Perry. 'Thank you.'

'Are you going to be around?' asked Tanya.

'No, knee deep in the case,' said Perry.

'That's a pity,' said Tanya. 'What's it like up in Inverness?'

'I'm sorry,' said Perry.

'Inverness. What's it like? Always thought I might get a job up there. Nice place. Good-looking men.'

'You never wrote. You said nothing.'

'I haven't been divorced for that long, Perry. It's been a year. And you were gone. I thought, well, I thought it would be hard to go back. I thought, will he be different? Will I be different? Do you get that, Perry? I have fears. Same as you. But you walked in that door, and it was just you again. I made a mistake. Am I too late? Is there someone else?'

Perry stopped for a moment. 'I don't know,' he said. 'I'll be honest with you, I don't know.'

'It's a long way up if there's no hope. It's a long way up if there's only a little hope. But with a little hope, I might make a move.'

Perry wondered what to do. Then he strode forward, bent down to Tanya at her desk, and kissed her on the side of the cheek. 'There's definitely a little hope,' he said. 'Good to see you again.' He turned and walked back to the door, and turned back to Tanya. 'And thank you for that.'

'A little hope?'

'Maybe more,' said Perry, and smiled as he walked out the door. As he disappeared back out to his car, thinking about phoning his boss, Perry felt something he hadn't felt for a while. Were things looking up?

Well, there's a little hope, he thought. *Just a little.*

Chapter 06

Emma Johnston was enjoying her first term as a teacher in Tiree. The class size was small. Yes, it was intimate, but it was also fun. Island life was suiting her. She was well known to everyone but also could find places to get away from it all.

Tiree was located to the southwest of the Scottish mainland, far enough away that you were out of contact from family without notice being given. She was benefiting from this life. Having had a poor marriage that ended in divorce, she just wanted time away from it all, doing the job that she loved, teaching primary school children. Today they were taking the kids to the green—a large pasture of grass where they would have sports events. Games with traditional egg and spoon, beanbag races, partner races, and the like.

Emma had also floated the idea of rounders and she was looking forward to it on a day that was fairly bright, if brisk. It was that time of year in Scotland when the weather could be great; it could be rough; it could be anything. Yet maybe that was true all year round. But the brightness today had made her smile, and the kids were in excellent form as they headed over to the green.

Alongside her was Mrs McGaw, an older woman of maybe fifty-five, now with white hair. She was out in a skirt, unlike Emma, who was in her leggings and t-shirt. That being said, Mrs McGaw would take part as best she could, but she wasn't in her prime, like Emma.

The kids assembled on the grass, Emma giving them a short briefing. They started with some races, simple running up and down. And then they had the egg and spoon and the beanbag race. It was while they were doing this that she noticed that something was up with Alex. Alex was a young child of only six years of age, and he was very quiet. Nothing was wrong with that, but Emma soon noticed that Alex was observant.

If anything happened in the class, Alex would see it. He might not tell you, but he would note it. When the class goldfish had died, Alex had spotted it.

Slippy, as the class had named him, had been the goldfish for at least six months. When they'd gone in that morning, Emma had fed the goldfish, and it certainly was alive, for it was eating. In the middle of class, however, she had seen Alex staring. And when she'd followed his eyes over to the tank, Slippy was on its side.

There had been tears that day. Distraught children who had paid no attention to the fish had broken down. But not Alex. Alex watched every detail of how the fish was removed and then the tank was cleaned, and an empty tank put back. When they got a new goldfish, Alex had explained the difference in size between the two goldfish. He said he couldn't give an estimate on how long he thought this one would take to die. That had cracked Emma up.

Right now, Alex was not interested in the games that were going on. Instead, he was sitting down looking over towards the beach, just to the north of the field.

'Well, Alex,' said Emma, 'your turn.'

Alex stood up, did his run up and down the field, got back into line and sat down and stared off in the same direction. While the running was continuing, Emma wandered over and sat down beside Alex.

'Are you okay?' asked Emma.

Alex didn't answer but continued to look off. Emma crouched down behind Alex, looking to see where he was staring at.

'What is it?' she whispered.

'Beach,' he said. 'Something on the beach.'

Emma stared for a moment. There was something on the beach. He was right. She wandered over towards Mrs McGaw.

'Alison, Alex has just pointed out that there's something on the beach over there. Looks strange.'

Mrs McGaw followed Emma's pointing finger and nodded. 'It is, isn't it? Maybe it would be worth a look. Do you want to go over?' she said to Emma.

'Maybe better if we both went.'

Mrs McGaw looked round and saw the janitor for the school who she called over. She then brought out a selection of juice and fruit, getting the kids to sit down in a circle to pass it out.

'Peter,' said Emma to the janitor, 'could you sit here a minute? There's just something on the beach I want to have a look at.'

'I'll have a look at it, if you want.'

'That might be a better idea,' said Mrs McGaw. 'I'm not the best on my feet anyway, and that sand out there can be quite awkward. You go with her, Peter.'

Peter was in his thirties, with straight black hair and a rather colossal frame. Despite this, Emma was quicker across, and got down onto the beach first, with Peter following her. As she got closer, Emma could see what looked like something flapping in the light breeze. She speeded up and spotted a coat on top of some rocks.

'Just a coat, Peter. No big deal,' she said. 'I'll just pick it up and bring it over. Leave it here and somebody else will come looking after it.'

For a moment, Emma thought about picking it up. And then she thought it looked rather damp. There had been a little rain, but not much. In fact, it was more like drizzle. But the coat looked sodden.

It was black and neatly made, with an almost woollen texture to it. She reached down to pick it up, but found it to be damp and heavy. She lifted her hands off it. They seemed to have a crimson tinge to them.

'Peter,' she said, calling after the janitor who had turned back, 'you've got a bag on you or something? This thing's filthy.'

Peter reached down into his pockets, pulled out a black bin bag, and began walking over to her. He rolled the bag out, opened it up, and held it in front of her as she went to pick up the coat. She tipped it into the black bag, but when her hands came away, both had heavy stains of red on them.

'What the hell's that?' blurted Peter.

'Sodden. The coat feels almost liquidy—damp, you know. We had that drizzle.'

Emma suddenly had a horrific thought. She rubbed her fingers across her thumb. It couldn't be, could it? She reached down and touched her lips to her fingers. It was an irony taste.

'It's not blood, is it?' she said to Peter. She turned and looked around her. How did she find a bloodied coat out here? Then she saw something else on the rocks.

'What the hell's that?' she cried.

'I don't know,' said Peter. 'It doesn't—is that definitely blood on your fingers?'

Emma's heart thumped, but there was an inquisitive side to her that would not let this go. She turned and started marching towards the figure she saw on the rocks further away. But Peter wasn't following her. He was still holding the black bin bag with the coat inside of it.

'I might need a hand.'

He was coming slowly now, but with great trepidation. Emma strode on. What would she do if it was a body? What would she—she froze. She could see a face. A face pointing up to the sky. Part of her wanted to run towards it, to confirm her suspicions quicker. Part of her wanted to turn and run. She didn't know what to do. Instead, she kept approaching, slowly.

There was a pair of black shoes, followed by a pair of jeans. Above that was a white t-shirt, except it wasn't white. Not all of it. Large parts of it were now covered in blood, especially up towards the neck area. She scrambled round the rocks and got a close-up view of where a neck had been ripped open with a knife. At least, it looked like a knife had been used. There was a clean cut across the neck, but a gaping hole, too. There was blood on the sand and on the rocks. Some of it mingled with the light drizzle. Red was running.

'Bloody hell, Peter. Bloody hell.'

Peter was approaching now, holding the black bag in front of him. But as he got closer, it fell from his hands. The coat fell out partly to the front. And Emma realised that it had taken most of the blood that had come from the neck. She looked back at the face of what was maybe a forty- or fifty-year-old man.

He would have been quite pretty in his day, she thought. He had a slightly effeminate look to him, especially with the eyes shut. Emma stood for a moment, the light wind blowing past her but feeling like a cold January chill.

She shivered and sighed. *What on earth? Here? Only a stone's throw from the school. A good throw, but still, only a stone's throw. And when? Had she been teaching? Had this happened while she had been in school with the kids? And how? Here wielding knives in Tiree, of all places.* Part of her wanted to run. But something else within her came to the fore.

She was standing over the body of maybe a middle-aged man with a gaping wound in his throat, blood everywhere. She couldn't let the kids see this. Emma turned to look at where they should have been sitting, eating. But they weren't. They were coming over now. With Mrs McGaw.

'What are they doing, Peter?'

He turned and saw the children running. Peter put his hands up.

'Don't! Don't come here!'

But the kids were taking it like a jest, because he didn't look like he was in control, like he was being authoritative. Instead, he looked nervous, panicked, like there was something he should be hiding. And yes, there was something he should hide, but he needed to be more demonstrative.

Some kids had now run ahead, racing past Peter, and Emma ran forward, scooping a couple up.

'Back! Everybody back! Back to the green!' said Emma. 'Nothing to see here!'

But she'd missed a couple, and now there was screaming.

'Mrs McGaw, round them up. You need to take them back,

back to the building, back inside.'

'Why? What's wrong, dear? What's up?' said Mrs McGaw.

'There's a body!' shouted Peter. 'There's a dead body!'

Some kids started to shout and yell. Some wanted to run forward to see it. Others wanted to run away. Panic was ensuing. Emma was losing control of them. Mrs McGaw had gone white.

'Body?' she said. 'What do you mean?'

'Enough!' said Emma. 'We have to get them out of here. Round the kids up. Peter, come on.'

One kid looked up at Emma. Emma's hands were outstretched, trying to corral them. But there was blood on her hands.

'Did you kill him, miss?' said a voice, and then there was more screaming.

'Get everybody back,' said Emma. 'We need to get them all back and we need to get the police out. No time to lose,' said Emma.

Inside, her heart was pumping, and it took the next five minutes to corral all the kids and keep them moving back. The front doors of the school were open, and as they streamed in, the canteen lady was stepping out.

'We're not ready. I'm not ready for lunch. You're early. Why are you early?'

And then she saw Emma's hands and screamed.

Emma ignored her, ploughed on through to the office, picked up the phone, and dialled. It took a moment for her to explain, to give the location, to make the call handler understand what was happening. She stayed on the line, passing on what information she could. When the call was done, she placed the receiver onto the cup with the phone and collapsed back in the chair beside the desk.

Emma looked at her hands. The blood was still on them. She felt sick rise up her throat and tears streamed from her face. She physically shook at the thought of what she'd just seen.

Slowly, she stood up, turned and walked to the nearby toilets and washed her hands in the sink. The water turned pink, running away from her. She scrubbed and scrubbed until she realised her hands were no longer red. But she was still scrubbing, still wanting to rid herself of what had just happened when Mrs McGaw came in to find her. Emma was hunched over the sink, tears flowing.

Chapter 07

Tiree was having one of those days. It was momentarily bathed in sunlight, then the clouds would roll across the sky, dropping their delivery of rain for half an hour before the sun would be back out. It was March, so it wasn't as warm as it could have been, but the sunshine was always pleasant after the long winter. The helicopter set down on the lush greenery around it, and Hope stepped out, keeping her head down from the blades above. Ross was with her, and they'd come over immediately, only waiting for a previous helicopter run, allowing Jona to go ahead of them. It was unlikely that anybody responsible for the murder of the man on the beach would have left by now under public transport. The ferries had been alerted with local police recording who was on them.

A car arrived to pick up Hope, and along with Ross, they proceeded up to the green, where the children had been engaged in their activities. Once there, she was met by one of Tiree's officers.

'Your colleague's arrived. We've helped her set up in the school. Children are all off now for the day. It'll be a couple of days, I suspect.'

'Well, it's not easy. It's not like you get something like this here very often,' said Hope. 'Glasgow's a bit different. Inverness too.'

'Well, whatever we can do to help,' said the officer. 'I've pulled together a brief list of what we did and how we did it. That's available here,' he said, handing Hope some notes. Hope gave Ross a nod, showing he should go with the officer and start going over the detail of what had happened.

Standing on the green, Hope looked around the beach area and could see makeshift tents up. Walking towards them, she felt the buffeting of the wind and, for a moment, almost felt she was going to slip. But she stopped herself, breathing in deeply.

There was a kind of light-headedness about her. For a moment, she looked for a seat, but there wasn't one. She tried to crouch down. The difficulty with that was she couldn't bend over fully, or at least didn't want to. She found that more and more. The arrival inside of her, slowly growing, meant the pressure on bladder and other parts of her body were developing more and more.

The light-headedness was getting too much. She let herself fall backwards onto her backside, and sat there for a moment, breathing in deeply. And then she saw someone running over. She put her hand up, indicating all was okay, but the figure kept coming. It was dressed in a coverall suit with its head covered with a hood. But that soon flew back. Judging from the size and the colour of hair, Hope knew who it was. With anybody else, she would have been able to turn round and say, 'Just leave me, I'll be fine.' But that wouldn't do for Jona.

'Are you okay? Will we get you inside?'

'I'm fine,' said Hope. 'Just feeling a little light-headed at the moment. I'll be okay in two minutes. Just let me be.'

'Are you sure?' said Jona, arriving, and taking Hope's hand. Then Hope realised she was checking for a pulse.

'I'm fine. Okay? It's just what is.'

'Okay,' said Jona. 'When you're ready.' Jona kneeled down beside her, and Hope gave a nod. She went to speak, but there was a little breathlessness, and so she remained silent.

'While I've got you stationary,' said Jona, 'I've made facilities up in the school. It'll do for the moment, and I'm checking the body. The body's got another book with it. I'm just getting the area photographed. I'll let you see the body, then we should be able to move it up to the school.

'I can do a bit of further investigation there. I'll see about removing the book here and taking it up first. The gentleman's in his fifties. Throat slashed. Looks very similar in that sense to the previous one.'

'Was he slashed? Somebody from behind, from in front, attacked or defending himself?'

'I would say, held strongly and the blade coming in from the front but the person being behind almost holding the head. That would be my guess . . . looking at where the body's fallen and the amount of blood that was around the area.'

'Well,' said Hope. 'It's a bit strange again, isn't it? Public and yet not public. Out here, Tiree's not overpopulated. There's many people here, though, at the right time being so close to the school.'

'That there is. No indications of somebody being dragged to the place, though, but the tide's been in and out, so footprints, that sort of thing, have gone. However, the body's on the rocks, just up enough off the tide again. It was going to be found. It wasn't a case of killing someone and hoping that the water would take the body away. This is deliberate. Somebody's leaving them here for us.'

'To get out to the rocks,' said Hope, looking around, 'especially if you come up to the road, you're going to have to walk past the school. You're going to have to be in this area. I suppose you could do it at night, but—'

'Runs a gigantic risk of being seen,' said Jona, 'similar to the last one, and yet you know at some point somebody's going to see it, because the school's close by. The golf course was close by last time.'

'Give me a hand up,' said Hope.

Jona reached over and pulled her. When Hope was about halfway up, she was clearing Jona's height, and Jona's pull became less useful. Hope staggered for a moment onto her feet and then sucked in a couple more breaths.

'Let's walk over,' she said, 'slowly.'

'The rain's been a pain,' said Jona. 'On one minute, off the next. But the local guys did well. They got it all covered over. A mix of tarpaulin and other things but at least it's helped preserve the body better than it would have been.'

'You think there's going to be any issues with the book?'

'Shouldn't be. As I say, it's in a zippy. It's there for you. Deliberately.'

'Have you looked at it?' asked Hope.

'Haven't removed it. Just letting them finish photographing, then I'll take it up for you. And I'll let the others move the body up behind us.'

They walked down onto the beach, Hope taking it easy. They made their way across to where some sheeting was covering the ground. Jona stopped at the edge of some blue tarpaulin, pulling it back, but not letting Hope go any further inside.

'You can see enough from here,' said Jona. 'Interestingly enough, there was a coat left over there. I think they must have taken it off him. It looks like it would fit the man. I'll obviously have it checked, see if there's anybody else's markings on it, or DNA, or anything like that. But I'm suspecting it's from the victim, because he hasn't got a coat on.'

'So why take it off? Why?'

'I don't know,' said Jona. 'Maybe it just got in the way. Maybe when he struggled, he got free for a moment. I don't know.'

Hope continued to look at the body, the gaping neck wound, probably caused by a knife.

'Same knife, would you say?'

'Certainly similar. I can't be certain until we get into the lab and get a proper examination of both bodies, but I would say this is probably the same knife. Certainly a similar mode of execution.'

'You mean execution as in—'

'Yes, not just the way they did it. An actual execution. This looked like an execution.'

'You bring someone to a point, then you kill them. Why wouldn't you kill them earlier on? Because you're coming to make a point,' said Hope.

'Exactly,' said Jona. She turned round to a man who was crouched down underneath the tarpaulin, photographing the body. 'You done?'

'Yes,' he said. Jona reached over to the body and pulled out a zippy bag containing a book.

'*The Gravedigger's Wife*,' said Jona.

'Seriously? *The Gravedigger's Wife*?" Get out,' said Hope.

'No, *The Gravedigger's Wife*. Why?'

'That's a K.F. McGrubbin book,' said Hope. 'Another K.F.

McGrubbin book. Story about a man who had something to do with killing people and burying them. He was the gravedigger, and she was the wife. She's the one that finds him out or something. Been a long time since I read it. I was sitting on a beach somewhere.'

'Oh, aye. Checking out the men instead of reading the book. That sort of thing, was it?' said Jona, teasing her.

Hope stopped for a moment. Actually, it had been back in the day.

'Let's get a proper look at it,' said Jona. 'Come on. Up to the school.'

Together the two women walked a not-too-short distance over to the school, speeding up towards the end to beat the rain. As the pitter-patter started on the roof of the building, Jona laid the book down on a table and began to glove up. She cleaned an area of the table down before taking the book out and placing it carefully on that area.

'Yep. It's *The Gravedigger's Wife*, all right,' she said. 'I'll just take a quick look through it, see if there's anything else inside it.'

The book was pristine, and had obviously been bought for the occasion. Jona flicked through it. She halted. 'Got a highlighted section here,' she said.

'Which bit?'

Jona pointed to a paragraph in the middle of the page. And the words 'just another corpse' had been marked by a yellow highlighter.

'"Just another corpse,"' said Hope. 'That's a statement, isn't it? But a statement for what?'

'List of bodies, list of jobs. Is it about somebody digging graves? I mean, the book is *The Gravedigger's Wife*. You're the detective.'

'Any more there, though? Are there any more lines?'

Jona flicked through the book, but there wasn't. There was a knock at the door, and Hope turned to see Ross entering the room.

'I had a word with the local guys. We're all good. We'll start a trawl. I'm going to check the port and the airport. Same again here as with Barra. See who's come in, who's gone away. But the guys say that there's been nothing unusual. Nobody reported. It's back end of winter coming to spring. You don't have that many visitors either. Any that come are generally noted. Relatives, family.'

'I'm thinking that it's got nothing to do with anybody that's visited,' said Hope. 'The book's *The Gravedigger's Wife.*' It's another K.F. McGrubbin, Ross. Got a line in it this time. It says, "just another corpse."'

'Why bring them here, though?' said Ross. 'If you were going to kill somebody, and you weren't actually residing here, why would you bring them here?'

'I don't know,' said Hope.

'It makes little sense,' said Ross. 'It'd be easier to kill them on the mainland or wherever else you find them. It just doesn't make sense.'

'You're wrong,' said Hope. 'It does make sense. We just can't see it yet. There is a sense in this. A definite sense. A story, a tale. Whether they're trying to spin that tale to us, or it's for their own rhetoric, for their own reasons, I don't know.'

Hope turned to look outside the window, and for a moment she thought a shock of red hair went by. She stopped and took a breath.

'Excuse me a minute,' she said. 'I think I need to go outside.'

The queasiness was coming back, and Hope stepped through the door, looked around and saw the children's toilets. She ran through the front door, then into a small cubicle with a half-sized toilet, got down on her knees and vomited. After a few minutes, she brought her head back up, took a deep breath and flushed the toilet. This was getting annoying. She grinned and looked down at her tummy.

'You'd better be worth it, little one,' she said.

Getting back up off her knees, she went over to the sink, washed her face, and dried herself down with some paper towels. Rather than go back in to talk to Jona and Ross, Hope stepped outside the building for a moment. As she did so, she thought she saw a flash of red hair disappear by the end of the building. She shook her head.

What was going on with her at the moment? She certainly wasn't running on all her full cylinders. Maybe she should talk to Macleod about that. Some women struggled with pregnancy all the way through. Some women coped without a great deal of problems. Everything she'd read about it showed such unique experiences. Maybe if she wasn't right, she should step back a bit. She was, after all, the DI. Not the DS or DC.

She was the investigating officer and needed to be fit. She sucked in some more of the sea air before stepping back inside and joining Jona and Ross back in the room.

'Okay,' she said. 'We do the trawl. Get who you can. I know it will not be easy. And Jona, get what results you can to me about the body, about who may have touched it, any contamination, anything at all. As quick as you can.'

'It's going to be awhile,' said Jona. 'Stretched as it is. We are equipped to go out to far-off places. But we've now got two places quite far apart, not easily connected either. I mean, we had to get the helicopter to get us over here quickly.'

'I appreciate that,' said Hope. 'Quick as you can. This won't be the last one and I'm not happy with people being executed on our watch, almost too easily.'

She looked at Ross, who gave a nod and went to leave. But as Hope looked out the window, she saw a shock of red hair again, almost as if someone had been there looking in.

'Ross, can I have a word?'

Hope stepped outside the room, letting Jona get on with her work, and Ross looked up at her with concern.

'Alan, tell me truthfully, okay? At the moment, I know I'm struggling a bit, fitness-wise. I'm having morning sickness, and I'm a bit out of breath occasionally. Is it affecting my work?'

'Not as far as I can tell at the moment.'

'If it does,' said Hope, 'tell me, okay? It's more important that I'm fit, or I stand down, and someone else takes over, than I carry on. I don't want to be proud about this.'

'Of course,' said Ross.

'And Alan, just to let you know, I think I'm seeing things. I've seen a shock of red hair on the move. Like a woman. I haven't clocked her fully, just the red hair moving away. I don't know where that's coming from. My head's spinning. I don't—'

'Stop,' said Ross. 'Susan, she said she was seeing red hair back on Barra. Convinced of it. Disappeared off after it but didn't find anything. I thought she was just being overzealous. A little jumpy.'

'You're saying that—'

'I'm saying we might have the same person on Barra. Especially red hair. You flame tops are not that common,' said Ross.

'Flame tops?' said Hope. 'You make it sound like we're some sort of strange folk. It's just a hair colour.'

'Yes,' said Ross, 'probably didn't phrase it in the best way.'

'No, you didn't. Just keep an eye on me, okay, Alan?'

Ross nodded and disappeared off to his duties. Hope remained. Red hair, somebody around. She needed to call the team together. There was a trail of books now, two bodies, similar execution. She had Perry off chasing things up in Glasgow, she had Susan over in Barra, Ross and her here, Macleod up the road, and Jona dancing between murder sites. It was time to pull everyone in and make sure they were on the same page, and line up where to go next.

Chapter 08

It was the following morning before Hope pulled the team together online. Ross had advised he would set up his laptop to communicate with everyone in the small Tiree hotel they were staying in. Hope was grateful for this, for when she woke up ready to go down for breakfast, she felt like she didn't want any.

She then spent the next half an hour running backwards and forwards from her own bathroom to her bedroom, and she eventually made it down for breakfast. She struggled to eat anything but knew she had to keep her strength up. Ross stared at her with a look that said, 'Are you sure you're all right?' But she ignored him. She was good. She could do this.

It hadn't helped that she had received a call the previous night from John asking how she was. She, of course, said she was fine, but he could hear the lie in her voice, and he'd been unsettled by it. In the end, she told him she wasn't fine, but she was coping, and Hope wasn't sure if that allayed his fears, or simply built them up even more.

The hotel provided a small room in which Ross and Hope sat with a coffee in front of them, ready to begin the meeting. As usual, Ross was the first one online, hosting the meeting, and it took the others a while to log into it. Susan arrived next, followed by Perry. But Macleod, as ever, seemed to struggle, and there was some other face there who he was thanking before he appeared online himself.

'Thanks for coming, everyone. I'm going to start off the meeting by just pulling together what we know and where everyone's at. Perry, you settling yourself down in the sunny south? What's happening?'

'That's the first time I've ever heard Glasgow being described as a sunny destination,' said Perry, giving a bit of a laugh. He relayed his tale of searching through the station.

'Regarding the deceased's picture, people don't seem to want to talk to me,' said Perry. 'That's not normal. Although I say it myself, I get on with people. I may not be the best looking, but I can approach people and get out of them what I need. Old Perry here can work with anyone, but nobody seems to talk to me, especially the old ones I used to know—people who would have passed me by, but always dropped a word to me.

'I got frustrated by that, so I went to talk to a retired inspector I worked under. Inspector Campbell remembered the man in the photograph as Desmond Barraclough. He worked in forensics for a short while and was medically retired because of a bad back. I'm going to see if I can hunt him down. Well, his history and life, obviously. I've got several addresses to go to, old ones, because nobody seems to know about him anymore. Or at least nobody seems to be prepared to tell me.'

'It might be to do with the case we're on,' said Macleod. 'Emmett's just worked a case that could be involved with this. Even if it isn't, Glasgow, at the moment, is not on the best of terms with me, and you lot working for me will get the brunt of that. I apologise, but that's the way it is.'

'What do you mean, "a case Emmett was working on?"' asked Hope.

'Just a connection which may produce the reaction that Perry's getting,' said Macleod. 'Beyond that, I have no substantiated evidence to say that the cases are tied in. But never say never.'

Slightly cryptic for Macleod, thought Hope, but there was no point pushing him because he clearly would give nothing more with that response.

'Keep going,' Hope said to Perry. 'Go through the addresses, see what you can come up with. If he retired under medical issues, find out why. I know it says bad back, but sometimes the reasons are beyond what's written.'

'Will do,' said Perry.

'How are you going over there, Susan?' asked Hope.

Susan Cunningham was sporting her blonde ponytail and in truth, looked a little jaded. She'd been left on her own and was running the operation over there. The islands sometimes had fewer resources. Although staff were always helpful, you tended to be working cross-agency with others from either the fire service, coastguard, or even ambulance pulled in.

'All we've done here is not producing anything substantial. Nobody had seen our murdered man, Mr Barraclough, before his body was found. Everything is coming up empty. I don't think anyone's holding anything back, because there's a good amount of rumour flying around the town. That kind of thing usually digs up somebody seeing somebody somewhere. But there's nothing.'

'Tell me a bit about the red-haired woman you went after,' asked Hope.

Susan looked a little embarrassed, but she continued. 'Well,

I kept seeing a red-haired woman every time I looked around, just in the background, not a prominent figure. So I looked to follow and eventually lost her down a couple of alleyways. I spoke to Ross, but he said it was probably nothing, getting a bit overzealous.'

'I saw a red-haired woman here,' said Hope. 'Not close up, too quick to actually get a description, but definitely red-haired.'

'Really?' said Macleod. 'Anything to do with the case you think, anything tied in with our deceased people?'

'No,' said Hope. 'Doesn't show like that. I'm thinking possibly an interested reporter, but quick on it if she's over here with me as well.'

'Very quick,' said Macleod. He dropped into a thoughtful pose Hope recognised.

'You may as well tell people what's happening here, Ross,' said Hope.

'So far,' said Ross, 'it's similar to what Susan's saying on Barra. Nobody reports anything about our victim or about any other strange people about. Small places, Barra, Tiree. People who aren't normally here get noticed.'

'So, what does that mean?' asked Hope.

'We've got beach locations,' said Susan. 'That could mean that they're coming on shore from the water. Also, you've had a victim on Barra, you've had a victim on Tiree. How do you get from one to the other quickly? You certainly don't do it by public transport. You'd be all day doing it. We're saying that the person isn't here to begin with, hasn't been about the local community. Have they been abducted from somewhere else and brought here? Easiest way to get to the islands without arousing suspicion is in a boat.'

'Agreed,' said Macleod.

'So what?' said Ross. 'They're grabbing them, stowing them underneath and then bringing them ashore to kill them?'

'Jona said it's the same knife,' said Hope. 'And by the way the bodies fell, possibly the knife was used from behind across the throat.'

'That's quite ritualistic, or certainly a consistent method,' said Macleod.

'It is, but why bring them here?' said Hope. 'Look at the books. The books seem to be a message. At least to somebody if not us. But why not just dump them all in the same place? Why run around? Why do it in a pattern?'

'Well, Barraclough,' said Macleod. 'It's pretty straightforward, isn't it? I mean, Barraclough. Barra.'

There was silence on the call for a minute.

'Pretty straightforward,' said Perry. 'But it works. So where was he found on Tiree? Are we looking for somebody called Tiree?'

'It's a bit odd for a surname,' said Ross.

'Where else have we got there?' asked Macleod.

'He was killed on the beach in Tiree,' offered Susan.

'I'll look into the names around here,' said Ross. 'I mean, there's Balevullin Beach, but it wasn't that beach. Clachan Mor nearby. Balevullin's the biggest place. The beach itself, I'm not sure what name we even have for it. It was Tiree Primary School that was beside it. Though they were all over on a big piece of grass, called the Green, I believe.'

'But he was found on the beach, Ross,' said Susan. 'Need to get that beach name.'

'Keep those names in mind, Perry, when you're searching for Barraclough. In case you meet anybody with similar names,' said Hope.

'I will, but I'm thinking also about the books. Why *Two's a Squeeze*? What's that about? Why pick a particular title? It's got to be to do with the titles, hasn't it?'

'There was a marked section inside the latest book,' said Hope. 'They highlighted "just another corpse" but the book on Tiree was *The Gravedigger's Wife*.'

'Barraclough was in forensics,' said Perry. 'You don't think that's got anything to do with it? I mean, we're talking bodies. "just another corpse"—that sounds like Barraclough, doesn't it? If you work in forensics, you see them all the time.'

'But that's not the book that was given with him though, was it?' said Ross.

'True,' said Perry. 'Just speculating.'

'Why *The Gravedigger's Wife*?' said Hope. 'And *Two's a Squeeze*." I'm not seeing how these two are linked in at the moment. We need to have to have a look at it. See if we can work out what these book titles are.'

'Look,' said Macleod, 'the recent case with Emmett makes me think these book titles could have been tied in. It makes me wonder about them. I don't want to say anything yet because I don't want to change your investigation. It may be something completely different, but it's a thought. It's not proved yet though. I need to ask some questions of certain people. Your red-haired woman—I'll look into that.'

'Look into it?' said Hope. 'She was seen down here. You're not going to leave the office, are you?'

'Only briefly,' said Macleod. 'I'll look into it. I know it sounds clandestine, but trust me on this one. I also have a thought about these book titles. Don't talk to Emmett at the moment about the case he's just been dealing with. It was done on the quiet and it needs to stay on the quiet. I need to look at it, have a think. If necessary, I'll bring you all in. But when we do, you'll be running silent too on that issue.'

Perry was holding his hand up on the screen.

'What, Perry?' asked Hope.

'I don't want to come across as untrusting or anything, but what is it you can't trust us with? What is it you're not putting out there so we can think through it as well?'

'Perry,' said Macleod, 'forty-eight hours. If you do as your inspector said, I may get more things that could tie into what I'm looking at. But trust me; don't follow up on what I've said until I say to do it. Don't take it anywhere except in your head and mention it to no one.'

'Forgive me, sir,' said Hope, 'but I'm inclined to agree with Perry. We're a close group up here, in Inverness. We may be all spread out, but you don't tend to be like this. You don't hold things back.'

'It's a safety issue,' said Macleod. 'That's all I'm saying. Don't talk to Emmett about it, or Sabine.'

'Fine,' said Hope. 'But I want some answers when it comes back.'

Macleod raised his eyebrow.

'Please,' said Hope. 'You know I trust you. We all trust you, but this isn't you.'

'No,' he said. 'It is me; it's just the circumstances are slightly different. I will ask some questions. I'll come back to you.'

'Good,' said Hope. 'Everyone else, Ross and I will finish up here. Susan, I'm not sure how much else you're going to find out there. Wrap it up and get ready to move. We'll work out where you are at that point, but your idea about boats is a good one. Ross and you make sure you ask at the ports. Start asking for people who are working the coastline. Maybe the coastguards are good people to go to, the teams that operate on the islands. See if there're any boats kicking about that are unusual. See if we can match any. Perry, you know what to do. Go find me Barraclough. Other than that, people, anything else comes to mind, talk to me. Have a good day.'

She stood up and walked over to the window while Ross closed down the call. Her stomach was doing somersaults, but she didn't feel like she was quite going to throw up. What she did feel was motion inside of her. She was getting more used to this, this idea that something was alive in her. John had talked about it being like the film *Alien.* Her memories of that little creature jumping out in the film weren't really helpful for what was going on with her.

'You okay?' asked Ross.

'I'm good, Alan,' she said. 'Are you?'

'It's not like the big boss to be like that. It makes me think he may be digging up a hornet's nest or something. Also, "Don't talk to Emmett. Don't talk to Sabine."'

'Yes, I was hoping maybe I could steal them. Or maybe even Clarissa if this gets busier and more spread out.'

'Well, it's looking like Clarissa could be the way to go.'

'Yes,' said Hope. 'That'll be interesting.'

Ross raised his eyebrows but his smile said he knew what she meant. He left the room with his laptop, leaving Hope in the empty room on her own.

What was Macleod up to? She had a good idea when he said he was going to meet someone. But she thought he had handed the Anna Hunt gatherings to her. She was the DI now. It was her case. But then again, would Anna Hunt seriously come out to Tiree? If it was tied into the other case as well, though, Hope wouldn't know about that. She wouldn't be able to talk to Anna about it.

Anna was a slippery customer, but she was on the side of the good guys, Macleod had said. She prayed that the red-headed woman was not a foe, but a friend. Hope didn't enjoy working with the service. It wasn't proper policing when they got involved. Macleod was more comfortable with that side of things than she ever was.

Chapter 09

Perry was trundling along in his hire car, feeling a little off kilter. It wasn't normal for him to come to a place and to feel rejected by everyone, especially with such silent treatment. Yes, some people used to not like his smoking, but since he'd gone to Inverness, he got used to the idea of being one of the more friendly ones. He was a person people actually wanted to talk to.

Yes, they regarded him as strange, especially those who were still out the back smoking. Perry stood a few feet from them, not engaging at all in the cigarettes, but deep in conversation. That was the trouble with not smoking anymore. You missed out on that bit. That's where people gathered. Smokers were a notoriously great place for gossip. You found out so much about what was going on.

You paid for it, of course. Dying early from lung cancer and that. But wasn't the job all sacrifice? Of course, he was kidding with himself. And in truth, he wasn't annoyed at having given up the cigarettes. He was feeling fitter for it. Yes, he could do with losing a little weight as well.

But lately, when he'd thrown himself about to intervene

in fights or situations they'd been in, he had felt stronger. More energetic. It was also good that Susan was feeling more inclined towards him. Not that she'd ever switched off from him. They were always friends. She'd had such a hard time with the leg, and he'd tried to help.

Maybe he'd helped too much, maybe she needed space, maybe a lot of things, but she'd been warm to him recently, very warm. Friend warm, though. He always made sure to tell himself that, not to get carried away. If she wasn't interested in something more, that was fine. He'd live with that, but he didn't want her to be turned off from him completely.

She was nice to talk to, a good colleague, and they worked well together. Hope was obviously impressed with her, for she'd sent Perry off and left Susan to manage Barra. Perry had more experience by far. Susan was fitter and was learning so much from Hope.

And of course there was seeing Tanya just the other day. He'd have to park those feelings for now. Life would get complicated otherwise, and he had a job to do.

Perry had visited three addresses that day, old addresses for Barraclough, and none of them had given any information. The man had been quiet and moved away from the few people that still remembered him. The trail had led Perry to Hamilton, on the east side of Glasgow.

Parking the car, he trudged along the street, which contained small, old tenement housing. Arriving at what looked like a shoddy green door, he pressed the doorbell. When he couldn't hear anything, Perry rapped on the door with his hand.

Perry stood and looked up and down the street. It was a street like anywhere else in the greater Glasgow area. People going about their business in a place that was, well, not destitute, but would probably struggle to say middle class. Maybe it had been in its day, for Barraclough had been here, well, twenty-five years ago at least, if not more.

'Yeah, hello, mate. You all right?' said a man opening the door.

Perry smiled, as he always thought that broke the ice with people.

'Hello, I don't want to alarm you, but I'm Detective Constable Warren Perry. I'm not here to investigate anything to do with yourself. It's just that this house used to belong to a Mr Barraclough, and I was wondering if you knew of him, or anything about him.'

'No, never heard of him. Wasn't the guy we took the house off. And you say you're a detective?' said the man.

'Yes,' said Perry, pulling out his warrant card and holding it up for the man. 'I'm sorry to bother you. It's just he used to live here. I'm going round different addresses trying to find out where he's been and where he is now. That's all. As I said, it's got nothing to do with yourself, except that you actually live here now.'

'Well, you could try the lady over there. Number nineteen.'

'Oh, why?' asked Perry.

'She's lived here all her life. She's Mrs Brown, but her first name's Elspeth, I think.'

'Elspeth? That's certainly an old name but Mrs Brown, I'll stick with that. I don't want a young whippersnapper like me addressing her improperly. Thanks for your help,' said Perry, giving the man a shake of the hand and turning to walk across the street.

This door was brown, full wooden effect, and it had no doorbell, so Perry hammered on the knocker. He could hear movement in the house, slow, and rather than rap the knocker again, he thought he would give it time. It was another two minutes before the door opened, very cautiously, on the end of a chain.

'I'm sorry to bother you, madam. My name's DC Warren Perry. I'm a policeman. Here's my warrant card. I'm here to ask you a few questions. You've done nothing wrong. It's about someone that used to live in this street.'

His warrant card was snatched inside the house, but the chain was left on the door. *Clever woman*, thought Perry. But it took another five minutes before the chain was actually opened. He didn't rush the woman, instead remaining incredibly patient. And when she opened the door, she smiled at him.

'I'm sorry, Inspector,' she said. 'You see, I had to get my glasses to read your warrant card. They tell us don't open the door to people. There are scammers about, you know.'

'Of course, hen,' said Perry. 'Not a problem at all. Would you want me to stay here, or would you want me to come in to talk?' She handed him back his warrant card.

'Would you stay there?' she said. 'It all looks very genuine, but I haven't anybody with me, so I don't want to risk a man being in the house with me when I'm on my own.'

'Perfectly sensible,' said Perry. 'I'm here to ask about a Mr Barraclough—used to live in the street. According to our records, it was that house across there.'

'Yes,' said the woman. 'That's the Adams now. Nice couple, young. The lad's a bit noisy. But no, they came across one time when my light was on in the middle of the night. I'd forgot to switch it off. They thought something had happened. They came across to look in on me. Nice people.'

'Sounds it,' said Perry. 'Mr Barraclough. You said you knew Mr Barraclough?'

'Oh yes, Desmond. Desi. He was a quiet man, very quiet. I'm eighty, you know. So he was a while back. Quiet existence, very private man. If you passed him, he'd say hello but he wouldn't engage in conversation. Had a lot of the street talking about him because of that. When you live in a street, you want to tell people a little so they're satisfied that you are somebody normal and decent. But you don't want to tell them too much because that's your business. You know?'

'Yes,' said Perry, writing in his notebook. 'So his private existence, did it involve anybody else going in and out of the house? Did he have anybody living with him?'

'Lived on his own. Didn't have friends round. Didn't have many people come round at all, really. Nobody—can't remember anybody, actually. He was police, though. Crime scenes. Played about stuff like that.'

'He was a forensic worker in the police for a little while, yes.'

'He used to get lots of packages, though,' said the woman. 'I remember it because packages would arrive and it would often be the same delivery boy. He was a boy. I mean, yes, I'm sure he was maybe eighteen, nineteen, or twenty, but to me he was a boy.'

'Really? But there were deliveries?'

'Yes, packages. And it was the same man often. In delivery uniform.'

'Did he ever tell you what the packages were?'

'No. Very rarely, I think. In fact, I can't remember anything. There was another couple of delivery people who turned up occasionally. Same company, sometimes the same van, but they didn't go inside. That had always struck me. The street said nothing, but I realised. Why did this delivery boy go inside? And when I say he went inside, the van would be parked.

'And, well, actually, it wouldn't be parked here,' said Mrs Brown, remembering. 'The van was parked away and the guy would walk up with the package. He'd go inside and he'd come back out, sometimes two or three hours later. And the package wasn't at the right time. The other delivery people, they came morning or early afternoon. This was towards the back of the afternoon. Or sometimes in the early evening, but always in his uniform, delivering a package.'

'That's interesting,' said Perry. 'Do you know where Desmond moved to afterwards?'

'No,' she said. 'He was still in the force when he was here, and then I didn't remember him moving. He had a van come, and the stuff moved. But he didn't move it. Done it remotely, I think.'

'And you do not know where he moved to?'

'No,' said the woman. Perry looked down at the list of addresses he had for Desmond Barraclough. This was the end of the line. This was the last one the force had. When he moved from here, they didn't know where he'd gone. He thought for a moment.

'I'm going to show you something. It's a face. It's the face of a deceased man. Now it will not look gory or that, but the man in it is dead. So, I don't want you getting a shock. However, I'd like to know if the person in it resembled anyone that you saw around Mr Barraclough's.'

'Don't worry about me,' said the woman. 'I've seen dead people before. You don't live in a street like this for this long and not see dead people.'

Perry wondered at that comment for a moment, but he believed she must have meant that obviously people died, and the neighbours found them. At least he hoped that.

'Here it is,' said Perry. He held up the photograph of the man who was found in Tiree. The picture was cleaned up, basically showing the bottom of his chin up and didn't show the cruel gash across his neck. The eyes were closed, and the man looked very much at peace.

Taking the photograph off Perry, Elspeth pulled it close, then held it away from her glasses. She took her glasses off, moved it closer again and then put them back on. This ritual continued for the next two minutes.

'Anything?' asked Perry, trying to remain polite and cheerful.

'That could be the boy,' said Mrs Brown. 'That could be him. I mean, this man is bald and older, but cheeks, everything, facially it looks right. He looks right.'

'Size?' asked Perry.

'Average height,' said the woman.

'That fits too. Can you tell me about the uniform? Which delivery company it was?'

'Oh, they're not around anymore. Oh, McAdams? Maybe. They had an A. They had a big A on the side, on the sleeve. Brown, but orange across it. Like arrows across. Chevrons's the term,' said the woman. 'Chevrons, that's what I'm looking for. The van designs were the same, but they're not about anymore. I could be wrong with McAdams, but it was a big A.'

'And you say when he would turn up, he'd be in there a couple of hours and come back out, yes?'

'Yes,' said the woman. 'I thought about it, you know. Young lad like that, going in with Mr Barraclough, him being that bit older. Nowadays, people wouldn't bat an eyelid. And I think that's why they did it, how they did,' she said.

'You think they were having some sort of relations?'

'Well, back then you wouldn't have admitted to it, would you? You'd have kept it very secret. Even then, it was not a done thing. Not like today. Although, you know, depends where you are, I guess, even today.'

'Indeed, it does. Do you have any evidence of a relationship? Did you ever see them kissing or, I mean, a hug or anything?'

'No,' she said. 'Just seemed very, well, seemed to me to be the likely story. But of course, maybe he was a drug dealer, and they were dropping stuff in.'

Perry almost burst out laughing at this older woman, rabbiting through potential ideas of misdemeanours that Mr Barraclough could be involved in. But she was right. It didn't actually mean there was anything between the two of them. It could actually be an arrangement to move goods. After all, he was going in with a parcel. That was either cover, or that was shifting something through. Barraclough was forensics. Could he be involved in drugs? Maybe he had the skills.

'Well, thanks for your time,' said Perry. 'Appreciate it.'

He returned to his car and drove off to find a nearby coffeehouse, sitting down with his laptop. He delved off into his computer, scanning on the internet, looking for parcel companies of the past. It only took ten minutes. Anderson's - brown and orange and they were still going, although they looked very different these days.

Perry noted the address and decided he needed to tell Hope about this. He picked up the phone, made the call, and she advised him she'd be on the first plane down to him. He thought she would; Tiree and Barra were old news. She wanted to be at the front of the investigation, and this was a potential lead.

In truth, Perry didn't mind; after all, he'd get a bit of company. Perry began to write out names and places, and the titles of the books that had been discovered. What did they mean? What did they have in common? What were they referring to? He couldn't help but think of Macleod.

How was he linked in? He thought about Macleod's cases. Those he knew. Those he didn't, he'd maybe have to look up. Something had been up with the big boss. Just what was going on?

Chapter 10

'I have to say, you have an incredibly trusting wife.'

Macleod's ears pricked up, but he showed no sign of nerves. He was sitting on the shores of Loch Ness, at a small picnic table. During the summer, it may have been packed with tourists, but currently, at this time in March, it was empty.

There was a little brown bag sitting on the table, and inside was a flask and a couple of cups. There were also some cookies. Macleod lifted the cookies out, put two cups down on the wooden table, and poured black coffee.

'My Jane has no worries about me,' said Macleod.

'She's not worried that some woman might try to nab you?'

'No,' said Macleod. 'She knows I wouldn't walk away with anyone.'

'True, even if you wanted to,' said the woman. 'Too decent, too honest, aren't you?'

'You probably don't meet many people like that within your business,' said Macleod. He gave a wry smile as Anna Hunt sat down opposite him at the picnic bench. He pushed her coffee towards her.

'The cookies are quite good. My secretary recommended

them. I'm not particularly a cookie person myself.'

'You pulled me all the way here, to the banks of Loch Ness.'

'I have,' said Macleod.

'This must be serious then, especially as you've brought coffee. And cookies. It's not a quick word, is it?'

'I don't see why we can't be civil,' said Macleod. 'I know I was a bit quick off the mark last time—'

'Italy? You nearly got yourself damn well killed. You're lucky Kirsten was out there.'

'No, Kirsten was out there because I got her to come out there. So that side wasn't luck. I was fortunate that she got her backside into gear quick enough to stop me from getting killed before she arrived.'

'But you're out here on your own, calling me in. Something serious is up.'

'And you're here on your own. No driver, just you,' said Macleod. 'I'm right. Something is up.'

'You believe that? What do you think is up?' asked Anna.

Macleod sipped on his coffee. 'Any of your people watching my team?'

'Why?' asked Anna.

'It wasn't a tough question. I asked, are any of your people watching my team? Now, I know my team,' said Macleod. 'I know them well. There's no need to watch them.'

'Well, then you've nothing to worry about.'

'Are you watching my team?'

'We don't run a secret service where people come up and ask us questions and we just say yes or no. It's not how the business works. I'm not the teller at the bank.'

Macleod took another drink, then placed his cup down and stared at Anna Hunt.

'I don't enjoy playing these games,' said Macleod. 'You're evading me. I thought we had some sort of level of trust.'

'I sort of had before Italy. But there you go,' said Anna.

'Tell me if someone is following my team.'

'Why would I tell you? I don't tell people higher up whom I deal with what I'm doing half the time.'

'Tell me. Or I'll expose them.'

Anna gave a wry smile. 'I don't doubt your detection efforts. I don't doubt your competency as a police officer. In fact, I highly rate it. And I am keen sometimes to use it. But how are you going to expose my people? It's not what you do. It's not your—'

'Kirsten,' said Macleod. 'Kirsten will do it. And she'll do it gladly for me.'

Anna lifted her coffee cup and drank some of it.

'Kirsten,' she said. 'It was the biggest mistake we made about her. She's completely loyal. And don't get me wrong,' said Anna. 'She's loyal to the country. She's loyal to the idea of the Service. And that we're here to prevent bad things. Unlike some of the other members I could talk about. But her loyalty to you far outweighs even that of the Service. Of doing right.'

'Oh, she'll do it for me,' said Macleod.

'It's funny, isn't it? You saw me taking away one of yours and corrupting them, and yet I've probably given you back as honest and as decent a person, but with our skills. I think you won that one. I'm not sure you thought you were going to.'

'Well, it's a generous compliment, but are you following us?'

'Not specifically,' said Anna.

She took another drink of her coffee, and then she picked up one cookie and chewed on it.

'Your recent investigation has met with great interest in

certain circles,' said Anna. 'You have stirred a hornet's nest. A hornet's nest that means that my people have been asked to keep an eye on things.'

'In what way?' asked Macleod. 'As in report, or as in stop?'

'Oh, they don't put it like that,' she said. 'No, no, no. You don't ask my sort of people to take action and eliminate people. That's a decision we formulate. And eliminating the likes of yourself, or any of your people, is not a good thing. I hope you think a bit more of me than that,' said Anna.

'Maybe I do,' he said. 'But why haven't you just come to me?'

'And interfere in police business? No. Also, for two reasons. The people I work for, well, the people I report to,' she said. 'I work for the country. I work for the best interests of the general populace. Ultimately, those running the country are not always on the same line. I'm sure you'll agree with me. However, that aside, when they come and they ask me about something like this, I need to know what's really going on. I don't want to come and meet with you, generally, in case they think that I'm on your side.

'We often fall on the same side, Macleod, but I'm not on your side in that sense. But usually, we're both trying to get to some reasonable revelation of the truth and an ending that everybody can go on with and justice is generally served. Sometimes it doesn't always work that easy for me. Maybe certain people high up are watching and they asked me to keep an eye on you. Or they've asked me to remain clear.

'What that means is that certain untoward things may happen to you and I'm meant to turn a blind eye. Well, their problem is that I'm not on their side. They were used to dealing with the old boss of the service, Godfrey. Godfrey would have looked at someone like you, Macleod, and not given two hoots if they wanted you out of the way. You're dealing with the trifling stuff. At least that was how he saw it.

'I don't see it that way. You mess with the trifling stuff, and the bad stuff runs to the top. When the bad stuff is at the top, I get asked to do things I'm not comfortable with and which shouldn't be done. Keeping away from you when something may happen to you is, well, one of those things. I believe your new DI was in Spain. I have contacts in Spain and there was an attempted hit at a bus stop.

'Now, my colleagues in Spain, or friends, to be more accurate, are not happy about what went on out there. They have relayed certain information to me. It gives me worries. You can't have British police officers simply being taken out. So, I am not watching your people. I am watching over your people, and I have set up investigations. That remains between you and me. If you want to tell your people not to worry about the person who's looking out for them—'

'The redhead,' said Macleod. 'It is a redhead, isn't it?'

'One of them is. Well, I'll tell you what. I'll have a word with her. Who spotted her?'

'Susan. Susan Cunningham was the first one. And then Hope. Hope thought she was away with it. Ross told Susan that she must be imagining something, but Susan doesn't imagine things.'

'In a few years, if you don't want her, send her my way.'

Macleod raised his eyebrows.

'I'm short on numbers,' said Anna. 'There's been a reshuffling of the Service that I took over. Getting it back on track and clearing away the deadwood is not easy. I could do with good people. In truth, I could do with Kirsten back.'

'Should I talk to Kirsten regarding what's going on?'

'I don't know what's going on,' said Anna. 'I know you're investigating. I have heard stories about the two bodies in Barra and Tiree. And the cover-ups. You have seen things within the police force. I'm looking higher up. I have got nowhere yet. People higher up know my people. And they don't wield power over the Service without having a good idea how it runs and how they keep the Service out of their own activities. They were daft enough to put a polite comment my way, as if to warn me to stay out of it. They wouldn't have had to do that with Godfrey.

'But they don't know me. They really don't know me if they've done that,' said Anna. 'Don't worry, I'm on your side. If you get anything else that you need to tell me, tell me. Don't hesitate. I'll keep an eye out for your people. But there's more than one group involved. There are lots of things going on here. And it worries me. It worries me because it isn't the good guys against the bad guys. There isn't a general consensus of the right and the wrong.

'Around this business, there was wrong on both sides. Real wrong. So, watch your back. I'll try to watch it as best I can. But you're going to have to watch your own as well.'

'Are my team in trouble? Are they likely to be? They took a potshot at Emmett.'

'Inspector Grump was very lucky. Or I heard he was very observant. That was on Spanish soil. They'd be more reticent to have a go on British soil. But don't think that they won't. Be very aware, Macleod, what's going on. Be very careful and watch who you trust.'

Anna Hunt reached over and took one of Macleod's hands.

'I like you, Macleod. Can I call you Seoras?'

Macleod looked at her hand and back up to her face. 'I meant what I said about Jane.'

Anna laughed. 'I don't mean it that way. I like you. You're one of the good guys. I don't want to see anyone come to hurt you. I like Kirsten too, although she can be a pain in the neck. The world needs decent figures like you. The public needs cops they can look at and say, "that's a man dealing with the situation, a man getting involved and coming in on the right side. He does justice." The world needs that. UK needs that.

'And yes, maybe in another world, I might have meant something more by this, but that's what I mean by it. Take care of yourself. Know your friends. I'm one of them. You can ask Kirsten if you will, but I am one of them. Monitor your team. If they see anything untoward, if they see anything that even just looks a little off, make sure they tell you. Fire it to me if you think it's really worthy. If I find out what's going on at the top, I'll tell you. You won't be able to use it, but it might help you in your investigations. Do it on the quiet, okay?'

She sat back again, took up her coffee, drained the cup and put it down. 'I'm going to take another one of those cookies. They're rather good.' She went to turn away.

But Macleod called after her. 'Anna, if I may,' he said. 'Thank you. I don't need to talk to Kirsten. I'm a good enough judge of people. But by the way, she always says that about you. She trusts you. And when you trust somebody in your Service, to the extent she does, they must be okay.'

Anna raised the cookie to her mouth, bit off a bit, chewed it and turned and said, 'Very nice cookies. Bring them any time. And the coffee. Drop of milk next time, though.'

He watched her go, disappearing through the tree line, and then she was away. Macleod sat down again. He could feel a chill running through him. Anna Hunt didn't know what was going on. Anna Hunt was worried. How big was this? What had he got himself into this time? He shook his head. He'd bring Kirsten in. Keep her on the sidelines, at least.

Chapter 11

Susan Cunningham was sitting in a small office, acquired for her by the local Barra police, in a fairly downcast mood. The others had moved on. She was left behind, mopping up the crime scene and the general statements. Susan had joined the murder squad dreaming of being able to do more than this.

There'd be more action instead of searches, domestic abuse, minor policing, albeit these things were important. Less visits to schools and some really nitty-gritty stuff to get into. At the moment, this was like administration. Statements had been made, and she was trawling through them again to find out if anything mattered. Of course, a large part of detective work was that—trawling. It wasn't moments of inspiration; it wasn't charging around like a lunatic bringing down some ne'er-do-well. Instead, it was a simple grind, and she was grinding today. Grinding through the reports taken down by the police officers drafted in from the rest of the islands. Reports taken from the general populace of Barra. She had wondered what good it would do.

In Susan's mind, whoever had killed Barraclough hadn't been on Barra for long. Had they appeared quickly? Were they still in hiding, unbeknown to the population? It seemed to Susan that they would have come in from the outside and gone away again quickly. She didn't know how they did that. She wasn't sure. A quick run on the ferry, but then the ferry had noticed no one unusual. Could they fly in and out? After all, the team did not know who had done this. If they didn't know who did it, it was very difficult to assign any blame to a random passenger on the ferry or on the plane.

There were always private boats, of course. But again, difficult to tie down what had gone on and where. You got snapshots from people, and their focus was generally on the golf club and the beach beside it. Trying to remember somebody about town? There hadn't been anyone. According to these statements, there'd been no one extra walking around Barra who shouldn't be. Yes, the populace generally knew each other, but there were always visitors popping here and there. Nowhere could she find anything that seemed strange in these statements.

Susan put down the current statement and moved on to the next one. She scanned through it, a habit she'd picked up when having so many statements to do. Well, that was interesting. There was mention of a new motorboat in the harbour, but no name. Maybe they hadn't seen that name. After all, the names were only on the side of the boat. The person looking at it could have been looking from any angle, but they'd definitely mentioned a new motorboat. Given the method of the murder, Susan thought this could be important. Of course, it could be another wild goose chase.

She made a note, and then continued for another half an hour, scanning through the rest of the statements. With nothing else having come up, she decided she'd put her time to good use by tracking down this new motorboat. It'd probably just be somebody out fishing.

Susan put on her coat, exited her temporary office, and found herself out on the street on what was a cold and overcast day. A small town, Castlebay was subdued.

As she wandered down towards the harbour, she could see the castle sitting out there in the middle of the water. It was a stunning backdrop for a postcard, but not somewhere she quite wanted to go on such a chilly day. She'd rather this was all done inside, but then she chastised herself—after all, she had been the one complaining about the lack of action.

There were a couple of fishermen working on their boats down by the harbour, and she thought that was as good a place as any to start.

'Hello. I'm—'

'You're one of the detectives, aren't you? The blonde one.'

Considering Jona had black hair, and Hope had red hair, being picked out as 'the blonde one' wasn't a massive feat. But Susan smiled anyway.

'Yes, I'm the blonde one,' she said, touching her hair. 'Detective Constable Susan Cunningham. I wonder, can I ask you a few questions?'

'Of course,' said the man. He was in his forties, and quite a jovial chap. But she could see the other man at the far end of the boat looking over at him and giving a knowing smile.

Susan may be being accommodated because she was a young woman but it didn't bother her. They were making themselves free to talk. After all, it was her job to get something out of them.

'I was just looking through some statements and someone mentioned that there was a new motorboat recently here.'

'No,' said the man. 'I don't remember a new motorboat. Well, we've been out. We're not long back in. Weren't about when that man got done in over by the golf club. We're not long in at all. Try over there.'

'Who's over there?' asked Susan.

'That's Isla. Isla and her sister. They have a tiny boat over here. They come down to it most days. Been working on it. Getting it ready for the summer. They like to take it out and about on the islands. They'd be worth talking to. Down the harbour most days.'

'Thank you.'

'No problem, Susan. If you need any more information, you can come here. Always happy to help.'

Susan flashed a smile at the man. She was sure he'd be happy to help, but she was also sure if he didn't have any information, he'd still like her to stay and talk. She walked around the harbour, down to the small jetty where a rather petite yacht was gently bobbing on the water. It was tied to the jetty, and Susan carefully made her way down to it. There was a drill operating inside.

'Hello,' said Susan. 'Anyone home?'

A brown-haired woman in her forties popped her head out of the hatch that led inside.

'Hello. Who are you then?' asked the woman.

'DC Susan Cunningham,' said Susan, pulling out her warrant card. 'I'd like to ask you a few questions.'

'Is it about that murder?'

'Well, yes,' said Susan, wondering how much other crime happened in Barra that would warrant her being there. 'Can I ask your name first?'

'I'm Isla, Isla McIntyre. My sister Rose's inside.'

'I was told by one of the fishermen over there that you're down here working on the boat most days. Would that be the case over the last few weeks?'

'Yes,' said Isla. 'Getting ready for the summer.'

'So you would have had a view of the harbour most days?'

'Yes. That would be the case.'

'Have you noticed anything unusual? Any unusual boats?'

'It's winter. There's not been a lot up.'

'There was that one,' said a voice from inside the boat.

'What?' said Isla, shouting back in. A drill started and Isla shouted again. 'Put that thing off! Come out here!'

'Just getting the cupboard sorted. Be there in a minute. Who is it anyway?'

'Police!'

'Police? It wasn't us!'

'She doesn't think it's us,' said Isla, shaking her head and then climbing out onto the small deck of the yacht. Susan continued to stand on the pontoon, seeing it probably afforded more space for her, and seemed a safer option. Eventually, a blonde-haired woman popped out beside Isla.

'And who are you?'

'DC Susan Cunningham. I was just asking your sister were there any new boats around here over the last couple of weeks.'

'I see,' said Rose. 'There was that one motorboat, remember?'

'Yes,' said Isla. 'Motorboat. Just over there, wasn't berthed for very long. Think they were just coming in for supplies, and out again. Had some foreign name.'

'Funny symbols,' said Rose.

'Funny symbols, yeah; wasn't like our alphabet—you know, wasn't our alphabet. Strange.'

'Okay,' said Susan. 'Can you remember what the letters

were?'

'Oh, I don't know,' said Rose. She turned and made her way back inside the yacht. Susan could hear a drill starting up again.

'Not sure. Not sure I could tell you what the letters were. I mean,' said Isla. 'There were the shapes.' She drew in the air with her finger.

'Can I ask you to get Rose and come ashore a minute for me?' asked Susan.

'Is it important?' said Isla.

'It's a murder investigation,' said Susan. 'It is kind of important, yes.' She smiled. But really, she wanted to grab the two women and just haul them ashore. A couple of minutes later, she had them both sitting down on the dockside with Susan's notepad in front of them. It was on a blank page and she had a pen, handing it to the women and asking them to draw out the name. It took a while, and the sisters bickered back and forward, until eventually they presented four pages of Susan's notebook.

'I think this is it,' she said. 'That first one, that's what Rose thought. Then I said no and then we changed that bit. Then we looked at it and we thought about it upside down because we saw it from an angle and then we looked at it a different way and I think this is it.'

Susan looked at the letters in front of her. They certainly looked different. She stared at the symbols. Greek alphabet? Was that Greek? Certainly looked that way. Hellenic, that sort of background. She was no expert in languages, but she could always call on people who were.

Susan thanked the women, took down their number and walked back to her office. Making a coffee, she sat down and trawled through the internet until she found a Greek professor at the University of Glasgow and placed a call through to him.

'Hi, there,' she said. 'DC Susan Cunningham. I've got a word which I think is Greek, or one of the Hellenic languages. I'm sorry, I don't know all the different types. I was just wondering if you could identify the word for me and tell me what it means.'

'By all means,' said the man. 'What are the letters?'

'Well, I think I'd rather send you a picture. I've had two women who say this is the words that they saw on the side of a boat. So, I don't want to influence you by saying what any of the letters actually are. Give me your email.'

An email later, and Susan had sent a photograph of her notebook over to the professor.

'Right. I've done well with that. The name in English would be "Alecto." It's a name.'

'Alecto? Never heard of that,' said Susan.

'It's from Greek mythology. Have you ever heard of the Furies?'

'They were the people who punished, didn't they? Or something or other.'

'That's right,' said the professor. 'According to Hesiod, Alecto was the daughter of Gaia. And she was fertilised by the blood spilled from Uranus when Cronus castrated him.'

Susan was slightly taken aback. Greek mythology was a bit brutal, to say the least.

'Basically, Alecto is the sister of Tisiphone and Megaera. They're the three Furies. They've got snakes for hair, blood dripping from their eyes, and their wings are those of bats. Alecto's job as a Fury was to castigate the moral crimes of humans, such as anger, especially against others.'

'Say that again,' said Susan.

'Well, her job was to be like someone who sorted out those who had anger against other humans.'

Susan sat back for a moment. 'Anger against other humans. So if somebody did something, the Fury would step in and sort them out.'

'Well, in this mythology. It's very well known,' said the professor. 'It's part of the Greek myths. Everyone knows them. Lots of kids read them growing up. Of course, we don't tell the full story. It's rather sanitised. Greek mythology is gory. As I said, Kronos castrated Uranus.'

'Brutal indeed.'

'If it helps you understand, it's Alecto in English, or rather, sort of. The translation would be something like "the unceasing anger." That's how you would describe the Furies—the unceasing anger.'

Now that interested Susan. When people put names like that on things, it was usually for a reason. You named your boat *Sunshine*. You named your boat after a place. Named your boat a positive thing. But 'the unceasing anger,' that was different. That spoke of revenge.

She thanked the man, closed the call, and then phoned the coastguard. She asked them to see if it was registered anywhere, knowing that they would have records of boats. It took them half an hour before they came back. There was no 'Alecto,' either in the Greek version or in the English. There was no 'Unceasing Anger.' No record of this motorboat. Susan sat back in her chair. The trawl may have worked. She might have dug something up this time. She'd need to contact Hope.

Chapter 12

Hope McGrath arrived at Glasgow Airport. Before she could get out to the arrivals area and meet Perry, she had to divert to the bathroom, morning sickness once again overcoming her. By the time she met Perry in the arrivals, she looked somewhat gaunt.

'Are you okay?' asked Perry.

'Fine,' said Hope. 'Just a little morning sickness. It's nothing. Now let's get going.'

'You should be taking it easy,' said Perry.

'Perry, if I want advice, I'll talk to my midwife. You just focus on the case in hand, okay? I don't need every man mollycoddling me.'

'Okay,' said Perry. 'Just trying to look after you.'

'I have a man for that. I've already left him at home,' said Hope. 'Let's go.'

Perry drove Hope over to Anderson's deliveries. He had contacted the boss, a Mark Lancombe, and arranged a meeting for that morning. The offices were smart and modern. Mark Lancombe, a big man with black hair and stout shoulders, shook Hope's hand and could almost look her straight in the eye without looking up. She could feel the bile in the back of her throat as she spoke to him.

'Thank you for seeing us, Mr Lancombe. I'm DI Hope McGrath, and this is DC Warren Perry. We're investigating a murder, well, a couple of murders actually, but one thing we'd like to know is about a former employee of yours. He used to visit a man called Barraclough back in the day at this address.'

Hope furnished the address to the man. He looked at it.

'We don't have the name of the delivery person, but he was a young lad then. Mr Barraclough was a degree older. We're trying to track down who he was.'

Perry produced a photograph—the body found on Tiree, cleaned up slightly so that the face was prevalent. Mark Lancombe stared at it.

'You're really asking the wrong person. Given the age of this guy, I'd say it's a few years ago he was doing these deliveries, so what, twenty, thirty? Best person to talk to is my mother. She would have been in charge then with my father. He's gone, and she's in her seventies, but she might be able to help you. I'm afraid I could look up records, but we don't have the faces, you know? She'd be a quicker route for you. Why don't I give her a call, tell her you're coming?'

'That would be excellent,' said Hope. 'I'd appreciate that. May I use your facilities, just while you're making that call?'

'Of course,' said the man. Perry watched Hope disappear. When Hope came back in, after once again requiring to deal with her morning sickness, she could see Perry's worried look. She gave a shake of her head, hoping to placate the man, and then received instructions on how to get to the house now owned by Karen Lancombe, Mark Lancombe's mother.

Perry drove them out to a smallish estate outside Glasgow, set at the foot of hills. Hope thought it was quite the retirement patch. The house was modern looking, and had a long winding drive up to it, which Perry negotiated. On arrival, the pair rang the front doorbell and were greeted by a manservant who advised them that Mrs Lancombe was expecting them. They were taken through the house out to a conservatory at the rear, where Karen Lancombe welcomed them.

She was a small woman with white, tight, curly hair, but a big smile. Hope wasn't sure if she wore dentures or not, but whatever, they certainly beamed at you.

'My son says you might require some information from me about our company and some former employees. Absolutely, I'll help, but the memory's not necessarily what it used to be.'

'Thank you, anyway,' said Hope. 'I'm DI McGrath, by the way. You can call me Hope. This is DC Warren Perry.'

'Please,' said the woman, 'sit. Would you like a cup of tea?'

'Absolutely,' said Hope. 'I'd appreciate that.' Karen Lancombe picked up a small bell that sat on a tray beside her. On ringing it, the manservant who had led them in previously received instructions from her and disappeared off. He returned a few minutes later with a porcelain tea set. He placed a cup in front of Perry and Hope before pouring them tea and then offering them sugar and milk. There was cake beside it, cut into slices, and again, this was offered.

Hope felt she should wait for the ceremony to finish before beginning the actual conversation, lest Karen Lancombe be distracted at all.

'It's excellent cake,' said Perry. 'Superb'

Hope watched him almost guzzle the tea. One thing about Perry was he wasn't refined. Cheerful enough and certainly polite. But not refined.

'Mrs Lancombe, if I may, I have a photograph here, not overly pleasant, of a deceased man. I was wondering if you would take a look and see if you recognise him.'

'Of course,' she said. 'Anything I can do to help.'

Hope watched as the older woman took the photograph, held it up in front of her, and studied it. Hope saw her face shrink in, shock plastered across it.

'Do you recognise him?' asked Perry.

'Indeed, I do. Sorry,' said Mrs Lancombe. 'It's just, well, it's a bit of a shock. I mean, he's older here. A lot older, but . . . well, I wouldn't mistake him.'

'Who is it?' asked Hope.

'Sorry,' said Mrs Lancombe. 'His name's Peter Green. I remember him well. You see, he was a very quiet lad. A quiet lad with, well, a bit of a problem back in the day. He opened up to me once about—'

'A problem?' said Hope. 'What sort of problem?'

'Well, it wouldn't have been a problem nowadays,' said Mrs Lancombe. 'Back then, my husband, he wouldn't have tolerated it. You see, Peter Green was, well, we said gay back then. Homosexual's the correct term these days, isn't it? And I know nowadays it's all fine, but back then it wasn't. It really wasn't. And my husband would have kicked him out.'

'But Peter confided in you, did he?'

'Yes, it was one particular day. I think the banter had got to him. Somebody made a joke about being gay—not at Peter directly—I think it just highlighted to him the situation he was in. He was desperate for nothing to come out about it.'

'We think he was visiting a man called Barraclough. Have you ever heard that name?'

'No,' said Mrs Lancombe.

'Barraclough received a lot of parcels from you, or at least we think he did. The van that Peter used to drive was often parked outside his house, and Peter would disappear inside for a couple of hours, always at the end of the day.'

'Peter took the van home at night,' said Mrs Lancombe. 'He lived a fair bit out from the depot, and so rather than get the bus during the week, we let him just finish off the end of his rounds and keep the van out there. It worked out easier for everybody. The trouble when they came in on the buses was when we wanted them to come in earlier because the buses weren't that frequent. The train or the bus broke down and then you were running behind on your schedules. Much easier just to give them the van so they could just disappear off at night and bring it back. There was never any mileage out. They had to account for it. But then I guess if he was . . . was it Glasgow that the man was in?'

'Yes, it was,' said Perry. 'Hamilton.'

'Well then. That wouldn't have been a problem. Hamilton would have been on his way home, I believe, for where Peter lived. It was out that direction. We probably have some old addresses.'

'What happened to him?' asked Hope. 'I mean, obviously he worked for the company. When did he leave?'

'Well, that's interesting,' said Mrs Lancombe. 'That's interesting because I got friendly with him, because he was a lovely lad. He really was. And he had an interest in some of the finer stuff in life. Like this tea service. He would have enjoyed that. He would have recognised what it was. No aspersions to the both of you, but I feel I could have served you up a tea service from the supermarket and you wouldn't notice the difference.'

Perry burst out laughing. 'No,' he said. 'I wouldn't notice a thing.'

Hope reckoned she might have noticed the difference, but she certainly couldn't tell if the tea service she was currently drinking from was expensive.

'Peter noticed things like that. He liked the finer things in life. And so did I. My husband didn't. My husband was prepared to pay for them and would be quite happy with me telling people how he had spoiled me with getting stuff. But he didn't understand. Peter did.

'So we had a friendship based on that. I used to show him some of the items I got. Of course, he always acted in front of other people as if he knew little about it. It wasn't a manly thing in those days. And I guess he was worried that if he gave in on that, that they might have put two and two together. I don't know. Crazy thoughts when you think about it. Why would your understanding of porcelain and crockery have anything to do with your sexuality? The man was living in fear. Definitely living in fear. What would have people thought about being friends with me? If my husband ever found out, Peter would have been moved on.'

'But what happened to him?' asked Perry. 'You were about to say.'

'Yes,' said Mrs Lancombe. 'I lost touch with him because he had planned to go away with his partner. He'd told my husband he needed a holiday. But he told me, quite specifically, he was going away with his partner for a weekend. Now, I never knew his partner. But from what you tell me, it sounds like it was probably this person in Hamilton. That would make sense.

'He would never give me the name, you see. I guess it protected his partner if anything happened to Peter. Or if Peter got found out. Of course, if I had the name, my husband could have got the address and things like that. Anyway, he said he was going away for a weekend. North. North of Glasgow. He didn't say at the time what they were going for. And I didn't ask. I mean, you don't, do you? Somebody's going away with their partner. You don't say to them, "And what will you be getting up to?" You just assume it's, you know, one of those more intimate weekends. Anyway, he came back.

'He handed his notice in to my husband. He said he'd found something better to my husband. But that wasn't Peter. I mean, Peter was happy with his job. And even now, when you tell me, and I think about him using the van, that would have been difficult elsewhere. But he said to me, because he said he felt he owed it to me, he said that they'd gone away for the weekend and they'd done something bad. In fact, no, he said terrible,' said Mrs Lancombe.

'He looked a bit ashamed. I asked was it to do with his partner and he wouldn't say anything. So I assumed it was some sort of lover's tiff or something that had happened. I didn't like to ask too much detail. I made sure he got a decent payoff, though, which he thanked me for, and then that was it. Not quite sure where he went after that. I mean, I was not even his employer directly. I was his employer's wife. I know I worked in the office and I saw him about, and we weren't friends on a deep level. I'm not sure how many people were with Peter, just the way he was. It's a shame, though,' she said looking at the photo again. 'To see him like that. What happened to him?'

'Well, he's been murdered,' said Hope. 'I don't want to say too much else at the moment. Still in the middle of an inquiry. But he's definitely been murdered. We will need those addresses, though. Any contact you've got for where he could have been.'

'I'll just go get you that,' said the woman, standing up. Hope thought she could see a tear in the woman's eye.

'Are you okay?' Hope asked her.

'Yes, dear. I'm fine. It's a bit of a shock when you see someone like that. Dead, you know. Brought back a few memories. A nice lad. Really pleasant lad. Got on well with him. Such a shame.' She wandered off out, and Perry looked across at Hope.

'When she gets the address, we need to follow it up. See where else it goes. Peter Green,' said Perry, 'murdered beside the green.'

'He was, wasn't he?' said Hope. 'Barraclough and Barra. Peter Green. What were they up to, though?'

'*Two's a Squeeze, The Gravedigger's Wife,*' said Perry. '*The Gravedigger's Wife*, referring to Peter Green. Peter Green, who was in a relationship with Barraclough. But what grave? Grave digging. "Two's a Crowd." "Just another corpse." I think these two have got something to do with bodies somewhere,' said Perry. 'I don't know where, but it's got something to do with bodies. The boss was talking about the potential for what Emmett said. Emmett's case. I think you should press him on that. I think we need to go back on that.'

'Leave that with me,' said Hope. 'You and I need to chase this through. See who else Peter Green's connected to. If he is, there'll be another one coming. Trust me. There'll be another one coming.'

'Two homosexuals as well. You think it could be to do with that? Old school. The old lady here said it, didn't she? He was afraid.'

'Yes,' said Hope. 'But what about graves? Grave digging. I would certainly keep the homosexual side alive in terms of theories, but I think the grave one might be a better one. I think you're on to something with that, Perry.

'But we need to move quick. That's two of them dead. Books placed with them. This is a series of killings, Perry. Who knows when the next one's coming?'

Chapter 13

Gemma Masters was living the dream life according to her friends and other people. She was an expert on computer websites and could design a website for you to bring the punters in. Whatever feature you wanted on it she could provide. But more than that, she could suggest features that would assist you much more than you could ever imagine.

She'd had record success, but with all of that, she was an elusive figure. Previously, Gemma had lived in Edinburgh, but she had decided to get out of the city. At twenty-seven, she wanted to live the good life in the clean air and the wide-open outdoors. She didn't need a man; she didn't need relationship problems. Gemma didn't need a group of friends hanging on that would tell her what to do and when to do it. So, against all family advice, she had taken herself off to the island of Colonsay.

It was certainly remote and the small house she'd bought—which she'd renovated at a lot of expense bringing in people from the mainland to do it—was her dream pad. She had an office upstairs while downstairs she woke up with morning views that were second to none. The island provided a runaround too and for company, she had Jake.

Jake was a scamp, a year and a half old, but great fun—a collie dog. He seemed to embrace life, loved the outdoors, running around off the lead whenever she was away from any farmer's field. But his favourite was the beach. She would watch him sniff here and there around rocks happily, and out here in Colonsay, often it was just the two of them. Yes, this was paradise. This was away from everything.

This morning had been busy. She'd been working on a new website for a client from Edinburgh. There'd been a phone call with them, which took a good hour, but was only explaining some of the basic concepts of what she was doing. Some people were just thick, weren't they? That was the annoying thing. She designed this website, and they had no idea just how good it was. But if they were happy, they would tell others. And others would tell other people. And so, the business grew and grew.

She wasn't short of work. In fact, to a large degree, she was picking what she wanted, delaying people by several months at a time. Some people got fed up with that and went off for someone else. But that was fine because she was never short of business, never short of those seeking her services. Gemma Masters was on the way up and that way would fuel her hermit lifestyle. Just Jake and herself.

By the time lunchtime had come around, Gemma was ready for a break. She'd logged off from her computer, stepped outside of the office, and shut the door behind her. That was it. She wasn't going back in, having had enough of talking to clients for the day. She'd take out Jake for a walk, come back, do a couple of hours this afternoon and then she'd take him out again before curling up. Yes, curled up with a book, and

Jake at her feet.

She'd lose herself in some wild-eyed fantasy of a book until the evening when she'd light the fire and possibly spend half an hour talking to her mum on the phone. After that, she'd cook dinner, but she'd have to work out what to have. She liked to cook, liked to make something special. And she even made special things for Jake.

With Jake, there was always the debate of whether she should. Was it the best thing for him? But he seemed to enjoy them. Right now, he was wagging his tail, looking at her with his gleeful eyes, saying, 'It's time!'

Dogs seem to enjoy walking. For Jake, it seemed to be his entire essence. As much as he loved lying at her feet, Jake wanted to be out and about and free to run. Gemma didn't quite understand it, though she had a similar passion—if the weather was decent.

She enjoyed being out in the open, too. Today was looking like it was going to be a good one. Cold but clear. She grabbed her jacket from the hook in the hall and wrapped herself up in it. With a bobble hat on her head and a scarf around her neck, she strode out into the brisk air. Jake raced off ahead of her.

She didn't need to keep an eye on him. He'd be fine. Running here and there and then coming back to her, just to make sure she was keeping up. Colonsay was a dream and Gemma was living it. Solitude. Yes, there were people on the island, and they said hello whenever they saw Gemma, but they were good enough not to intrude her space.

It was good to talk to them in those few moments when she sought company, but generally, they left her alone, understanding that the quiet life was what she wanted. Whenever they came up to 'Writer's Block,' as she had named her abode, they would ring the doorbell, pass a few words, see if she was ready for talking. If not, they'd wish her a good day and calmly go on their way. They were all out here for a reason, after all.

Gemma was heading down to the beach at Whistler's Bay. It was far enough away from everyone else, and she liked to spend an hour having Jake run back and forth on the beach. Sometimes she built a sandcastle and he would smash through it and she swore he almost laughed. Of course he didn't—he was a dog. But he would stare up at her, begging her to build the next one. So much so that she enjoyed it.

Whistler's Bay and the beach there were thought of by Gemma as her private spot. Her own bit of paradise away from everything. Her private beach. But today, she grimaced as she saw a motorboat lying off the shore. What was it doing there? Well, not that far off the beach, either. Gemma continued to grimace as she walked closer to the beach.

And as she got down to it, she called out, 'Jake, back!' just in case anyone else was down there. People could be funny with dogs, and Jake could be super friendly. However, not everyone wanted a dog to jump up on them, and Jake, not being around that many people, hadn't learnt that yet.

'Jake!' she cried sharply. She saw him running back towards her, ever so briefly. Then he stopped, and he turned and hared over across to some rocks on the beach. He was bolting, going quickly like he'd got a scent of something. Gemma shook her head, stood her ground and shouted, 'Jake! Jake!' But Jake wasn't for turning back. *Stupid dog,* she thought.

No, he wasn't. He was just a dog, just doing what they do. He just needed to understand that it wasn't appropriate to do this when there were people about.

She glanced over at the motorboat and saw it powering away

from the beach. Gemma sighed—well, at least, they wouldn't be about. She'd get the beach to herself, thank goodness, once she caught up with Jake.

'Jake, where are you, boy? Jake!'

She heard him bark, but the bark wasn't coming closer. She honed in on it, walking over towards some rocks. They were right up on the tide line. Just beyond maybe. As she got close, she saw Jake sniffing at something. And there was a thing in Jake's mouth.

'Come here, you,' she said. The dog went to bolt past her. She grabbed him, ever so briefly, by his collar. And in that moment, as she held him, she saw he had a book in his mouth. It was inside a zippy bag. But it was definitely a book. He struggled though, broke free, and tore off along the beach.

There was a gurgle. Or was it a cry for help? The noise came from behind the rock. Gemma turned, stepped over the larger rocks, and then let out a gasp of horror. She didn't know whether to step forward or to step back, and for a moment just froze, looking down at the scene in front of her. There was a man lying on the rocks, and his throat had been slashed, but he wasn't dead.

He was gurgling, not particularly loudly, more like the last throes, like he was on his way out. At the end, right before the body stopped twitching. The eyes were wide open, but they weren't moving. The body was fairly still, the occasional twitch, but all in all, the man looked like he was about to succumb.

Gemma decided to step forward. She reached down towards his throat and could see the gaping wound. She could see into a place of the throat that you shouldn't be able to. Blood had seeped out over the beach. Gemma reached down with her hands, at first not knowing what to do.

If somebody put a hole in his throat, should I not just cover it up? Because otherwise, the air was coming out, wasn't it? He could breathe properly then. Couldn't he?

She covered his throat with both hands, and they were immediately drenched in blood. Gemma looked at the red on her hands. She should phone someone. Colonsay was so far away. She needed to get somebody here. They need a helicopter to get him to the hospital.

Who did you phone? Coastguard, wasn't it? The ambulance couldn't get here. It would have to be the coastguard, the helicopter. She needed a mobile. Except she didn't carry a mobile about here. Why would she need a mobile? People didn't die out on the beach. This was Colonsay. This was quiet. This was remote. This was away from it all.

But this was like something you'd find on the back street of Edinburgh on a terrible day. Not on Colonsay on a cold, crisp, winter morning.

The man continued to choke. What should she do? Should she make a run for it? Back up to the house and call? Should she take him up there? Take him. Carry him. Get him to some help. Get the neighbours.

'Jake!' she shouted, looking over at the dog, but it was still haring about. It seemed to be throwing the zippy bag one way and then throwing it the next. What on earth was he doing with the book?

And she looked down again at the neck of the man. Her hands were as red as she'd ever seen them, blood dripping from them. *She couldn't carry him all the way back, could she? It wouldn't work. She couldn't do it. The motorboat could have helped, though, couldn't it?* She turned to look for it. It was continuing to disappear. Gemma stood up, waving her hands frantically, specks of blood flying off them as she waved them back and forward.

It wasn't coming back. She'd have to make it up to the house. She'd have to.

Gemma turned and started running hard for her house, leaving the beach, climbing back up onto the moor and racing towards her own home. Once inside, she made for the phone, hearing Jake coming in behind her.

She grabbed the phone, collapsing into a chair, and dialled 999.

'What service do you require?'

'Coastguard,' said Gemma. She could feel the blood dripping off her hands now, onto her clothing. It would be everywhere. She could feel herself beginning to shake, panic now taking over from the dutiful response that she'd given so far.

'Coastguard rescue. What's the problem?'

'I'm on Colonsay. Man on the beach. Throat slashed. We need to get him out of here. He needs an ambulance. He needs to go to hospital.'

'Say again?'

'Man with his throat slashed. He's got his throat slashed. He's . . .'

'Your position? On Colonsay. Whereabouts on Colonsay?'

'Whistler's. Whistler's Bay. The beach at Whistler's Bay. I've had to come to the house. I haven't got . . . well, I need the mobile. I'm not sure if I get signal. It's just me and the dog— and him. None of the neighbours are about. I could get them, but . . . we need a helicopter. He needs to go to hospital. He's got his throat slashed.'

'I understand. Stay on the line a moment.'

Gemma sat and watched as Jake came up to her. He still had the zippy bag with the book. Part of the book was now torn inside, his teeth having chewed their way through the zippy, which was ripped. Where on earth had he got the book from? There was a man lying dying. Why had he been reading? Why had he had a book inside a zippy bag?

'Helicopter is on its way. Is there anyone with the man at the moment?' asked the coastguard officer on the other end of the line.

'No, there's not. I had to come up to make the phone call.'

'Are there any doctors, first responders, anyone on the island that you know who can help? Helicopter is going to be twenty minutes at least, if not more.'

'I can see. I can ring around and get them to come down. Then I'll head for the body. Yes, I'll go to him. I'll be at the beach. I can wave and show them where it is.'

'Is there much room on the beach to land?'

'How much room does a helicopter need?' asked Gemma.

'Never mind,' said the officer. 'See if you can get somebody down there with first aid training, at least. We'll do what we can to get somebody else there. But the helicopter will have a paramedic on board.'

Gemma passed her mobile number and then grabbed the phone, unsure of just how well it would work when she was down on the beach. But she couldn't leave the man down there. She needed to be on the beach, point out where to go for the helicopter.

Quickly she rang round the neighbours, and although she couldn't find anyone with medical training, they said they would come down. She thanked them, and then went to wash her hands, but thought better of it. No, what was the best thing to do?

That man, he needed somebody with him. 'You need to get down there, Gemma. Come on,' she said to herself.

She saw Jake sitting there, looking up at her expectantly. The dog had no idea what was going on, did he? She turned and ran down the hallway to go back out her front door, but halfway along, she tripped over something and fell hard down on her shoulder. She scrabbled back to her feet and looked round.

Jake had obviously dropped it again. He'd dropped it. The book in the zippy bag was now lying in the middle of her hallway, a proverbial banana skin that caused her to slam hard into her own carpet. What on earth was the book doing with that man? What had happened? Gemma's head swam as she picked herself and headed out towards the stricken man on the beach.

Chapter 14

The body being discovered in Colonsay, Hope had left Perry to follow up on Peter Green. She was flown by a police helicopter up to Colonsay from Glasgow. It was a cold day and flying in the relatively small helicopter did nothing for Hope's morning sickness.

She could feel the bile in her throat coming up and down, the gaseous eruptions that she struggled to hold within her mouth. She wished it would all be done. Why was it that some women enjoyed the pregnancy? Some women got to almost bask in it. Hope wasn't basking in it. Hope was surviving it because of the little dream at the end. The idea of a child, of someone to hold.

She told herself to snap out of it as she gazed out at the clouds before they descended and set down on Colonsay. One of Jona's team came to meet her and took her down over the moors to Whistler's Bay, where Jona could be seen working. It was an unusual scene in some ways. Normally, when there'd been a murder, you would have the forensic unit and uniform all around it. A hive of activity. And in other places, more remote places, it looked sparser.

But this, this was as sparse as it got. There were only a couple of officers, Jona, and one other of her forensic team. They'd managed to place a tarpaulin up and create a shelter for the body. And while Jona was still dressed in her full forensic garb, Hope could sense that the woman was a little on edge.

'Afternoon,' said Jona to Hope.

'You all right?' she asked.

'I'm stretched here, truly stretched. Three bodies, three different islands. Do you know what it's like trying to get the wagon from one to the other? The ferries you have to go on. It's not like they just go from one to the other. You've got to get back over to the mainland, then come back out. It's not suited for what we do. Time is so important. You can lose so much.'

'You might notice the lack of police officers as well,' said Hope. 'I've got Susan still back in Barra. Ross is over on Islay. I'm here and I've got Perry chasing something up in Glasgow.'

'I'm short of people, too. Even the local guys. You don't get that many out here,' said Jona. 'They've come over on the boat and they're not sure when they're going back.'

'Just do what you can. And do it as well as you can. You always do,' said Hope. 'I'll have to muddle through. Then again, it might be part of the ploy. I mean, why would you kill people here? We know the deal with the last lot now. We have a Peter Green, which is why he was killed beside the green on Islay. Barraclough killed in Barra. But where's this?'

'This is Whistler's Bay,' said Jona. 'Maybe you're looking for a whistler.'

'Tell me what you've got.'

'Gemma Martin found our victim. She lives up in the house back there,' said Jona, pointing off into the distance. 'The woman's cut up. She actually tried to save him. He was still breathing when she got to him, but the throat had been slashed. Got her hands covered in his blood. Her dog was the one who found him. Unfortunately, the dog also ran off with a little book inside a zippy bag.'

'And the book was?' asked Hope.

'*A Hand on the Tiller*. You know it?'

'It's McGrubbin again. It's another McGrubbin book,' said Hope. 'This one, mid-level crime boss. He had control of everything that was going on, but he was under pressure with the commands being sent from above. It was all about him negotiating the two.'

'Looking at the throat,' said Jona, 'highly likely that the same knife's being used. Once again, somebody standing behind, cutting across the throat, almost execution style.'

Hope stood up and looked around her. 'Why here, Colonsay? A bay on the backside of Colonsay. There's no people. How would you know it would be found?'

'It is an inhabited island, Colonsay. There are several people. It would be found. And if you look at where they've left it on the rocks, the body's been left where it won't be washed away. Every time. It's very deliberate. Although this time, I believe it was quite close.'

'How do you mean?' asked Hope.

'When I was talking to Gemma,' said Jona, 'she said to me that there was a boat in the distance, a motorboat. It was like it had just been here. It was close by, but it just kept going.'

'That's why nobody's seen him. That's why nobody's seen our victims. Why they haven't been on these islands. Small island, lots of local people. Anybody new comes on, they would spot them. But they're not in amongst the community. They're being brought to specific places,' said Hope. 'Being brought, killed.'

'Killed? No,' said Jona.

'What do you mean?' asked Hope.

'When you kill someone, they just happen to be there. You follow them, you kill them. When you bring them somewhere and then do it, you're holding them. You must have subdued them to bring them here. That's execution.'

Hope turned away, sat down on a nearby rock. 'You're right. You're right. Captured and brought to a place and then executed.'

'If you're held from behind, it's a classic way to execute. Cut across the throat,' said Jona.

'So, the boat is bringing them here. Are they storing them up somewhere? Some other island? And then carrying them back and forth? The boat's not staying anywhere for long. Except it was in Barra. It was in Castlebay.'

'Maybe it ran out of something.'

'How hard would it be to hide a boat?' asked Hope.

'With all the islands around here? West coast of Scotland? Go to one of the uninhabited ones. Hide away inside an inlet, or cave. It wouldn't be that difficult. Plenty of little coves and places on the islands. You can stay out of sight. If you're self-contained, it's not a problem, is it? You've got all your food. Maybe you've already got all your victims,' said Jona.

'Something to think about, isn't it?' said Hope.

'What about the book this time?'

'Well, Perry has got the idea that Peter Green and Barraclough had something to do with graves. Hence, *The Gravedigger's Wife*. He doesn't understand *Two's a Squeeze* though. Peter Green may have had a lover in Barraclough.'

'Bit of an age gap,' said Jona.

'Yes, but also a secret love. Back in those days, you didn't let everybody know you were gay. It wasn't a thing that you did. You could really get persecuted for it. Much more than these days.'

'So what, somebody's killed him because he's gay?'

'No,' said Hope, 'I don't go with that. What's up is that the two lovers went away for a weekend, came back, and Peter Green told his boss's wife they'd done something terrible. I'm wondering if that's what it's all about. I don't know what it is, though.

'Emmett was on a case that Macleod thought might be linked to this. Seoras is being funny just now. I don't know. It used to be different. I used to work directly with him. We were a team, the two of us. He used to bounce a lot of stuff off me. It's my case now. Or it's Clarissa's case. Or Emmett's case. It doesn't work the same. I don't get the same closeness with him. But what I do know is he looks to be under pressure. He said something about Emmett's case possibly being linked in, but he wasn't sure. Or maybe he is. I don't know.'

'Well, maybe you need to have a word with him. If he's holding something back from you, it's serious,' said Jona. 'He's a deep man, but no one shows us all that which we don't want other people to see. Maybe it's something he doesn't want you to know. Something that will make you think ill of him.'

'Ill of Seoras? How can I think ill of Seoras? He's the reason I'm here. He's the one that brought me up through the ranks. Seoras backs me to the hilt. He—'

'That's the very reason he wouldn't want you to see it. He values what you think of him. Almost more than—'

'What?' said Hope.

'Well, I shouldn't say it,' said Jona.

'What?' demanded Hope.

'I think he wishes he was twenty years younger. He likes you in that way.'

'Get out,' said Hope. 'I'm pregnant. I'm about to have a baby with my man. He's never—'

'Of course he's never. He's too proper; he's too polite. And he's got Jane now. But he's got a fondness for you that goes beyond the rest of us,' said Jona. 'Remember, I got pretty close to him. We shared some stuff when he was doing therapy with me.'

Hope turned away. Inside, she knew it was true. It was uncomfortable, in the way that you had a scratchy sweater, because she knew she had a similar feeling for Seoras. The age, of course, the background, everything else, meant that nothing could, would, ever, should happen. But it didn't stop you from being fond of each other.

She felt a vibration on her phone and picked it out of her pocket. 'Speak of the devil,' said Hope. 'Excuse me.' She walked a little way away from Jona before answering the call.

'Hey, I haven't heard from you for a bit,' said Hope. 'You find anything out then?'

'I had a meeting with a friend of ours. The red-haired woman. Don't worry about her. She's looking after you.'

'Good,' said Hope. She was staring back up at Gemma Martin's house, and in the distance, there was a figure with red hair.

'Why am I being looked after, though?' asked Hope.

'I don't know exactly. Because our friends don't know exactly. There's been a change at the top with the Service. Anna Hunt is running it now. The person who ran it before apparently had a good relationship with certain high-up people, and was happy to bend to their will on things. Anna doesn't work like that. So Anna's investigating what's going on. The case I had with Emmett, she was deeply interested in.'

'So why is she interested in the case I'm running?' asked Hope. Her hand went down to her belly. She didn't like the Service involved. The Service acted quickly, decisively sometimes. People could get hurt, injured, in a way that the normal police force didn't countenance. The force's idea of public safety and that of the Service were two very different things.

'The bright side is,' said Macleod, 'that you have somebody watching for you, but be very careful.'

'We're stretched thin,' said Hope. 'I have got people off on their own here, and you're telling me to be careful. Can you give me Emmett? Emmett and Sabine? Or Clarissa. Give me a few more bodies.'

'I'm not bringing Emmett and Sabine near it. Not yet.'

'Why?' asked Hope.

'If the case that Emmett and Sabine were working on is tied to this, and they're in the middle of it, people will think we know more than what we know. Let us just keep working away. Somebody's telling us a story.'

'And the bodies are piling up with that story,' said Hope.

'Any luck on the recent one?'

'Whistler's Bay. *Hand on the Tiller*. That's the book. You tell me. I'm not happy,' said Hope. 'I'm not happy because we're stretched. I can't run a case like this.'

'You're going to have to,' said Macleod. 'This is bigger. This is spiralling. But we need a way in. We can't step out of line for it, though. We need to just go through the procedures until something breaks. Until something falls down.'

'I'm not following you,' said Hope.

'You don't know everything I know,' said Macleod. 'You can't possibly hope to follow what I'm saying. Keep going for it. What's your next move?'

'The bodies are being dumped ashore. They're using a vessel for it. Vessel *Alecto*. We need to find that vessel. It's out here somewhere. But it's not stopping in a lot of places. The coastguard doesn't know of it. So, we need to find it. If we find it, we might intercept things before the next lot happens. Unfortunately, it's not what we do well. We're going to have to talk to our coastguard friends on that one.'

'Agreed. What about Perry?'

'Perry's down in Glasgow. Peter Green, our second victim, has some former addresses given to us by his former employer. I'm getting Perry to check those.'

'You may need to pull people together,' said Macleod. 'I agree, you're too widespread.'

'Give me Clarissa. Give me Patterson.'

'No,' said Macleod. 'Not yet.'

'Why not?' said Hope.

'Like chess. You don't put your pieces into battle until you know they're being used in the right way,' said Macleod.

'I have absolutely no idea what you're talking about these days,' said Hope. 'I'll tell you when I've got more.'

She closed down the call, turned and stood and looked out at the sea. *The boat is out there somewhere. Bloody Seoras. Something is up with the man. This isn't him. Seoras shares with me. But right now, he's scaring the hell out of me!*

Chapter 15

Perry couldn't believe his luck, and it wasn't good luck. The boss had come down, and when she had arrived, they'd been treated to tea in porcelain cups, cake. Now she'd disappeared back up to another body; he was out in at the rough end of Glasgow.

In front of him were tenements, but they were badly run down. Coupled with the cold, Perry wasn't in the best of moods, as he began knocking on doors. The address he had was incomplete. Although he knew he was in the correct tenement, he wasn't sure which door he should knock on. It took him three goes before someone remembered Peter Green and sent him to the door across the hall.

The hallway had graffiti scrawled over it, and Perry wondered how people lived here. There'd obviously been no attempt to clean it up, but then again, maybe it would just be put back up again the next day. He'd seen this before in certain areas. Inside, some houses were done up as anyone would do their house—some immaculate—but the outside gave a completely different image. He wondered what he was about to get. Would he get anywhere? He wasn't banking on getting a cup of tea, or some cake.

Perry rapped on the door because there was no knocker or doorbell. It thundered inside the tenement, and he heard somebody swear before footsteps approached the door. The door slid back, and a woman stood in curlers and a dressing gown.

'Who the bloody hell are you? What do you want?'

'Forgive the intrusion,' said Perry, and produced his warrant card. 'I'm DC Warren Perry.'

'If he's been at it again,' said the woman, 'I'll kill him. I'll damn well kill him.'

'We may be on cross purposes,' said Perry. 'I'm looking for a Peter Green.'

'Peter Green? You don't want Jimmy?'

'No,' said Perry. 'Should I want Jimmy?'

The woman quickly turned, almost presenting her back to Perry. 'No, you don't want Jimmy,' she said. 'Peter Green, he used to live here.'

'So I'm told,' said Perry. 'You been here a while?'

'A good while,' said the woman. 'He gave me a piece of paper, oh, a long time ago. Here,' she said, as she pulled open the drawer of a small table in the hallway. 'Yes, this is it. Who did you say you were again?'

'DC Perry.'

'Well, you're lucky I've got it. He gave me it and I stashed it down at the bottom of this drawer and then, well, I haven't cleared this out in years. Still there though.'

Perry looked at the address. Glasgow again. Not that far away.

'Thank you,' he said, and took the piece of paper with him.

'You haven't seen Jimmy, have you?' said the woman.

'No,' said Perry, waving his hand and making his way back

to the car. He would head for another tenement. This was less than half a mile away.

The building on arrival, however, looked derelict. The last one he'd been to had definitely been occupied, despite the graffiti on the outside and the occasional badly hanging door or smashed window. This one looked like nobody would be in. From the outside, quite a few of the windows were boarded up, including the front door.

Perry walked round, eventually arriving at the rear of the property. The rear door was broken, hanging off to one side. Perry wondered if there would be rats here. He wasn't a big fan of them, but the entire building had that sort of feel about it. In fact, the estate did.

Maybe it was due for demolition, because there was no one here. Not even kids playing. Maybe they came round when school was finished, although there were plenty who didn't get to school. He wondered if there might be even some drug addicts inside.

Carefully, Perry picked his way across the back garden, as it would have been before it had become the current rubbish dump, and entered the hallway. He could see the other side of the boarded-up front door. The flat he was looking for was two flights up, and when he got there, he saw the door was lying open. Slowly, he pulled the door to one side. The smell of fustiness almost knocked him for six. There was a dampness in the air, but Perry wandered in, looking here and there. The front room had a large dresser in it, as well as an old TV. The sofa had been chewed by something.

Perry put on some evidence gloves, more to protect his own hands than anything else. He started shifting through drawers and found some paperwork with Peter Green's name on it.

Old bills.

He worked his way through the dresser, finding nothing of particular note, but demonstrating that Peter Green had been here. Evidence of daily life, things to pay, library cards. At the back of the dresser, he found what could almost be described as a secret drawer. He had to reach in, almost round a corner, and activate it, and the drawer slid out inside the cupboard. There were photos there, and he took them out to study them in a better light at the window.

As best he could tell, they were of Peter Green and Barraclough. None of them were in public places. Many seemed to be in a living room or a bedroom. There was nothing salacious in them. All just happy photographs. Yes, in some, they were hugging. There was even the odd kiss between the men. But it didn't look like they were anything but the joy of their relationship.

Perry thought back to those days, twenty to thirty years ago. Some of these photographs would have been enough to have the men pilloried and abused. No wonder he hid them away.

Perry wondered what had happened to the flat in the tenement. He placed a call into the council and eventually got through to a rather robust-sounding woman. He gave the address to her and asked for a history of the place.

'Most of the addresses there have for a long time been forgotten. The whole area is going to come down and be rebuilt on. We moved some of the last out, but Peter Green, you say? Ah, that address. We assumed it was abandoned. People just haven't got round to clearing it out yet. The whole place is going to get knocked down. Some new builds. New estate. That's the way it's going these days.'

But he must have moved from here a long time ago, thought

Perry. *Did he get chased out? Was somebody on to him? Of course, he was dead now. What had happened between living here and being deceased?*

He walked through to the kitchen and when he opened the fridge, he quickly closed it. There was a terrible mould inside it. Unbelievable mould. He wondered if that fridge had been opened in years. He could see the evidence of where the rats had been, and it gave him a chill.

Perry looked out the window across the rest of the estate, and then he heard it. *That was a footstep*, he thought. *There's nobody else here. The estate is abandoned. Nobody's about.*

He took a step back into the hallway of the flat, and he thought he heard something from inside the front room. Slowly, Perry made his way to the door.

Inside was a woman. She was tall, wearing a jacket with what looked like dark jeans. The woman had boots on, not with high heels though, sensible ones. She turned to Perry. There was a baseball cap on her head, a ponytail of black hair peering out the rear. She wore shades. And she had a scarf that was pulled up across her mouth and nose.

'Who are you?' asked Perry. 'And why are you here?'

Perry was surprised by the woman's speed. She was across the room in an instant, picking him up by the collar and throwing him back into the hall. His shoulders drove into the wall, causing him to let out a yell. Before he could fall, she had grabbed him again, spun him, and was throwing him back across the hall into the wall on the other side.

As Perry felt his body turn, he stumbled down the hallway towards the kitchen. Looking back, he saw the woman reach down for him, but a hand grabbed her shoulder.

She was grabbed and thrown up the hallway. The woman

before Perry now was smaller, dressed in jeans. She was compact, but she was clearly fit. Wearing a black leather jacket, her hair flowed out from beneath a beanie hat. But she also had glasses on, with dark filters.

Perry watched as the taller of the women came towards the smaller, throwing punches. But the smaller woman was lighter on her feet. She danced left and right, struck the other woman with two severe kicks into the midriff, before following up with a couple of punches to the face.

Perry heard the shades break and watched as a large looping kick sent the taller woman spiralling back up the hallway.

And then the battered woman ran. The smaller woman went to the doorway of the flat, then came inside and went to check the windows before coming back to Perry.

'Are you okay?' said the smaller woman.

'I think I am, thanks to you.'

The woman unzipped her jacket and took off her beanie hat, shaking out her hair. As soon as she removed the sunglasses, Perry clocked who it was.

'Kirsten Stewart,' he said. 'We've not really met, have we?'

'Macleod said I should keep an eye on some of you. I'd heard Hope was coming down, so I've been following you most of the day. Although she was heading north, that person didn't follow Hope. She stayed on you. She'd also been out to the other address, asking about Peter Green. A lot of people been asking about Peter Green.'

Kirsten reached down, giving Perry her hand, and pulled him up to his feet.

'So,' said Perry, 'she's from the side that doesn't know where he is or what happened to him. Not the ones that took him.'

'That's why you're still a detective,' said Kirsten, giving a smile.

'What does she want with me, though? I found some photographs of Peter Green and Barraclough. She must have seen them when she went into the front room. There's nothing else here. There's nothing—'

'That would confirm that you had tied Barraclough to Peter Green. You'd tied up the first two bodies,' said Kirsten.

'Yes, it would,' said Perry.

'Did she ask you anything? Did she threaten you? Did she look for information?' asked Kirsten.

'No. She threw me out into the hall. Was coming for me, I think.'

'Good job I was here,' said Kirsten. 'I think she would have destroyed those photographs and killed you. Somebody didn't want Peter Green and Barraclough to be tagged together. Certainly not confirmed to be together.'

'I'll call Hope. Make sure she knows about this.'

'She's tied up at the moment with Jona,' said Kirsten. 'I just spoke to Macleod. I won't accompany you. I will keep a distance. He doesn't want me to be seen. He asked me to look after you guys in case things got a bit hot.'

'You can walk beside me any time,' said Perry.

Kirsten pulled out her phone, put up an image of the body that had been found at Whistler's Bay. 'That's the latest one. Macleod sent it to me to see if I knew him, but I don't.'

'Well, you wouldn't. Not unless you'd played in the Glasgow Police football leagues. That's one of the guys who used to referee it.'

'What?' blurted Kirsten.

'He was one of the Glasgow Police League referees. That's David Funnell. I better let Hope know.'

'Get to your car and drive off. I'll watch you get in and, like I said, I'll keep a discreet distance. Take the photographs with you.'

'Of course,' said Perry. He disappeared into the front room, gathered the photographs, and came back into the hallway to say thank you again to Kirsten, but she was gone. Perry made his way back down to the car, got inside, and placed a call to Hope to advise her he'd recognised the body of David Funnell. *Whistler's Bay, Whistler's Bay*, thought Perry.

When he finished his call, he started up the car and headed back to his hotel room to clean up. He thought about Kirsten defending him, and he gave a smile. She was slightly younger than him, and he liked the idea of having this bodyguard walking around in front of him. Susan had mentioned Kirsten when telling Perry about Italy, although she hadn't gone into a lot of detail about her.

As he stood in the shower, cleaning himself down, he felt his head, where a slight bruise was coming out. Suddenly his thoughts changed from one of warmth towards the young woman who had defended him, to the sudden thought if she hadn't been there. *Things are getting too serious*, he thought. *You don't just take police officers out for finding evidence. What did these two guys do?*

Chapter 16

Hope McGrath sat on Colonsay in a room in a small farmhouse. It had good Wi-Fi and now, along with Jona, she would conduct a meeting with her entire team. Of course, they were all spread out, but thanks to technology, they could have a proper round table.

She let Jona continue to set up the meeting, awaiting everyone to join in as she sat down in the corner. Hope hadn't taken a chair, simply gone straight to the floor and had pulled her knees up tight—or as tight as she dared without crushing her bump.

She concentrated on breathing. She was feeling nauseous and Hope had been sick earlier. Pregnancy was meant to be a joy. That's what they always told you. 'Look at me, my lovely bump.' They didn't tell you about all of this.

Hope had gone off for about half an hour to John earlier on. And God bless him, he'd just taken it. He kept telling her she was doing well. But all she wanted was this sickness to be away. She had a job to do. And in truth, things were looking like they were getting themselves involved in something deep.

'I've got them all,' said Jona. 'If you want to come over.'

Hope nodded, hauled herself up off the floor, and walked

across to sit down on a seat beside Jona. There were many screens on the laptop now, and she could see them all: Macleod, Ross, Susan Cunningham, Perry.

'Evening everyone,' said Hope. 'As you probably know, we've identified, or rather Perry has, our body up here in Colonsay. His name's David Funnell. Perry can talk a bit more about him.'

'Thanks,' said Perry. 'He was David Funnell, an amateur referee. Used to referee the Glasgow Police Soccer Leagues when we used to have matches.'

'You used to play in that?' said Macleod suddenly.

'Yes,' said Perry, almost offended. 'I mean, it wasn't a particularly professional level. Anyway, David Funnell, he used to referee them, but he was also a civic leader in the Glasgow Council. As I remember it, he had a reputation for being hard on crime and demanding law and order. At the time, the McIntosh crime family was extensive, and this guy, Funnell, he was through the roof about them. He wanted them stopped.'

'The McIntoshes?' queried Macleod. 'I don't remember him being particularly outspoken.'

'You probably don't remember him much at all. He was a civic leader, but he wasn't one of the big ones. He wasn't the one you got on the telly. If you'd read the papers, if you'd read the reports from the council, you'd have seen him standing up every time, banging on and on about them.'

'Did you read those?' said Macleod.

'I did. I liked to know who was who,' said Perry. 'I was working in Glasgow, so I read all the way around it. What happened, how decisions were made. You could find out a lot of things that way. You could see the influences underneath the surface.'

'And you say he was outspoken against the McIntosh crime family,' said Macleod.

'Very much,' said Perry. 'Is that important?'

'What I'm about to say remains within the team. It doesn't go to anyone outside of here. The only other person you may discuss it with is Kirsten Stewart,' said Macleod. 'Emmett and Sabine have recently worked on a case that took them down to Pitlochry. It was to do with an old colleague of mine called Gavin Isbister. Now, we've discovered that Isbister was set up and got the blame for killing someone.

'The victim was looking to expose details about a certain group within the police back in the day of the McIntoshes. One of McIntoshes' men was killed up in Pitlochry and then the civilian who was investigating into all of this, Simon Matthews, was also killed. Isbister disappeared. They said it was suicide, but Emmett's investigations have found Isbister in the grave of the Simon Matthews, alongside the deceased.'

'Two's a Squeeze,' said Perry.

'Yes,' said Macleod.

'*The Gravedigger's Wife.* Do Green and Barraclough have anything to do with this?' asked Perry.

'I don't know. I get the feeling that somebody is trying to tell us that.'

'You went to see Anna Hunt,' said Hope to Macleod. 'Does she know anything about it?'

'No,' said Macleod. 'And that's what bothers me. Anna Hunt will know everyone who is operating in the UK. And certainly any groups. Sometimes groups outside the law are allowed to operate. Sometimes they have higher-up connections. Of course, it's never officially said. But then again, the Service is hardly official. Anna told me to watch my back when I spoke to her. She's worried that there are things going on she doesn't know. Anna's launched investigations,' said Macleod.

'Anna's launched investigations?' said Hope. 'Anna told you to watch your back. So what are we getting into here?'

'I don't know,' said Macleod. 'I really don't know. That's why I sent Kirsten. She went down to follow you, Hope. She said that she spotted someone tailing you. Except the person didn't follow you. They followed Perry on his investigations when you left for Colonsay.'

'If Kirsten hadn't been there,' said Perry, 'I'd have been dead. Somebody didn't want us to put Barraclough and Green together.'

'And somebody else did,' said Macleod. 'That's where the clues are coming from.'

'But why not just tell us?' said Hope. 'Why not just come to the police and say, "Look, this is the story?"'

'Because somebody doesn't trust the police,' said Susan Cunningham suddenly. 'Somebody wants to make sure they're understood. Trying to say they're not the bad guy in all of this, although they're killing people.'

'Don't see how all the books come into it,' said Ross. 'It's very cryptic.'

'No, it's not,' said Perry. 'They're constantly saying something to us. Don't you see it? *Two's a Squeeze*. It's the two bodies in the coffin. They're letting you know about that. *Gravedigger's Wife*. Barraclough. Killed on Barra. Peter Green. At the Green. On Islay. *Two's a Squeeze*. *Gravedigger's Wife*. Peter Green. Barraclough's partner. Digging graves. We're being told it's those two. They did it. They were the ones who put your friend Isbister in there.'

'And so, what about David Funnell, then?' asked Hope.

'Whistler's Bay,' said Perry. 'No mistake. He's the man there.'

'But the book that was with him, *A Hand on the Tiller*,' said Hope. 'It's McGrubbin. They're all McGrubbin books. That one was about a mid-level person, managing troubles from the top and the bottom.'

'Hang on a minute,' said Ross. 'How are they getting all these books? How are they getting these titles? Very convenient.'

'They're using McGrubbin's books,' said Hope. 'Somehow, for some reason, McGrubbin's books seem to fit. Don't they?'

'If you look at the titles, they're fitting what they want to say,' Macleod stated. 'There's got to be something in that. You could just pick books from anywhere. Leave a book with a title. There are so many titles in the world you could go for. Why be a specific author?'

'That title, *Hand on the Tiller*,' said Hope. 'That's a mid-level crime boss. Are they saying that Funnell was mid-level? It's Funnell above the last two. Are those two the gravediggers and Funnell's the guy at the top?'

'I don't know. I have no idea,' said Macleod. 'We've nothing other than what they're telling us to go on. But everything we've found out so far backs it up. Peter Green, Barraclough, clearly lovers. The idea they worked together, they disappeared up north, as said by Mrs Lancombe. A weekend and did something terrible, and he disappeared.'

'Here's a thought,' said Ross. 'If these people who've killed them knew that they'd done that, when did they know? You said you were down at Peter Green's in your early report,' Ross said to Perry. 'But that place had rats in it, done out. You think they've been after them for a while?'

'It's possible,' said Perry. 'I wondered about that. Why isn't there a new house to be grabbed from? Maybe we just don't know where they have been. Maybe they went to ground particularly well, Peter Green.'

'At the moment,' said Hope, 'we're getting stuff handed to us. I feel like we're trying to confirm what they're telling us. Somebody else is stepping in who doesn't want it confirmed. We have two sides here, one of whom Anna Hunt clearly is bothered by.'

'In fairness,' said Macleod, 'I think she's bothered by both, because she doesn't seem to know either.'

'Stories are clearly being spun, though,' said Perry. 'We've been going to Glasgow and not getting a good reception in places.'

'Sabine had the same,' said Macleod, 'when she went to investigate.'

'Maybe Emmett and Sabine could come join us,' said Susan. 'Then we would—'

'No,' said Macleod. 'No, that will not happen.'

'That's obviously your decision,' said Hope. 'But maybe for the team you could explain a bit more.'

'Emmett and Sabine were shot at when out of the country,' said Macleod. 'Perry's just been attacked. What I don't want people on the outside to know is that we have tagged this investigation in with Emmett and Sabine's investigation. We have two groups. One who's trying to spoon-feed us and lead us on clearly to some discovery about these people they are killing. There's somebody else there, trying to cut any evidence we find. And Hunt doesn't know who they are. The more we keep people in the dark about what we know, the safer we will be. For that reason, at the moment, Emmett and Sabine will not be seen with you. We will have distinct teams. The only connection is me.

'And that's okay. I'm the DCI, overseeing all three teams under me, but I won't bring Emmett and Sabine in with you. I also won't send in Clarissa and Patterson to help. I need them clear, just in case.'

'Just in case of what?' asked Hope.

'Just in case we need to investigate something else attached to this, and I need to do it really quietly.'

'We're overlooking one thing,' said Jona suddenly. 'The knife. I believe the same knife is being used each time to kill these people. They are being sacrificed. They are being ritually killed, in that they're being brought to a place and then slashed across the throat from behind. It's got a very ritualistic sense to it. These people are being executed, not just killed.'

'That speaks of a society. That speaks of a cult,' said Ross. 'Are we really saying that there could be a cult behind this?'

'A society's probably better. Cults don't operate so much in the dark. Not like this,' said Perry. 'This sounds like a high-level society. This sounds like—'

'This sounds like people taking the law into their own hands and operating above the level where anyone should operate,' said Macleod, clearly annoyed. 'But we can't go in too quick.'

'Clearly it's getting to you,' said Hope.

'Of course, it's getting to me,' said Macleod. 'They killed Isbister. They killed a friend. That man was good to me. He was an outstanding officer. They tainted his life. They tainted everything about it by killing him.'

There was a silence before Hope spoke again. 'Okay, I think the DCI has explained the seriousness of the situation. I'm not happy with us operating on our own anymore, even if Kirsten is lurking in the background. Let's work in pairs. Ross, get down to Perry. I want you to both investigate the contacts Peter Green may have had. See if you can link him into David Funnell. That's where they're asking us to look. So, let's go look. Susan, you join me. We're going to look specifically at Funnell himself. And his life.'

'I'll see what I can do,' said Jona. 'But in truth, we're having difficulty trying to get a lot from the crime scene. These people are good. They're not leaving a lot behind. They're leaving behind what they want to leave behind, namely the books. I'm trying to see if I can find where they were bought, but it's not happening. There's no commonality between them. They've probably been bought in many places. Even the zippy bags are slightly different. It's clever.'

'I will tell Kirsten to keep a watch,' said Macleod, 'but Hope is right. No risks. Be careful. Any issues, get out of there. If you can, keep yourselves in public; it's always safer.'

'The other thing we can look at,' said Hope, 'is why McGrubbin's books. We need to know why they're using the same author. Can we trace our killer through that? I'm not sure how.'

'If we could get the knife,' said Jona. 'That's another line of attack. I can look at the blade. But knives are more than just blades. If it's ritualistic, there might be something in the knife. Something about it.'

'These are all good,' said Macleod. 'Good ideas. But get to it. Get together. Stay close. I'm on the phone whenever you need me. I won't be coming down unless there's a dire need. Let this be your team's case, Hope. I need it to look like it's just a murder squad investigation. The moment they think I'm involved and I'm linking things together, we're in trouble. We become proper targets.'

'We keep Seoras at a distance,' said Hope. 'You've all got travel arrangements to make. Let's get together and get on with it.'

It was another ten minutes before Jona had left the room, taking away her laptop. Hope had spent them pondering what was coming.

During those ten minutes, her hand kept descending to her belly. Why now? Why this? Why this big? It wouldn't have bothered her before, but she had another life to think about. And as much as this little bundle inside her was causing her sickness and nausea, she already felt such a protective instinct.

Part of her wished Macleod would come down. Part of her wished Macleod would take over and she could just protect her own. But she was a police officer. And clearly, somebody had killed one of their own to cover up schemes. She was with Macleod on that. You didn't overlook that. You went for the people that did it.

Chapter 17

'What on earth is this?' said Ross, as he met Perry at the pickup point at Glasgow Airport.

'This little baby was less than a grand. I'll sell her again when we're done.'

'Why have you bought a car?' asked Ross.

'What Macleod said. Hire cars you can trace. Put them on the expenses. This'll be fine. I'll sell her again for what I bought it for. She's quite good too.'

The car was a pale green, and Ross could see the rust on either side.

'Are you sure she's legal? I mean, she's got an MOT?'

'She's got leather seats inside,' said Perry. 'These were good cars in their day. I like it.'

Ross took his bag and threw it into the boot before getting into the passenger side of the car. He turned and saw a smiling Perry. 'Where to?'

'I want to go back to the disused property. Peter Green's. You said you searched it. Did you search it fully? Did you get everywhere in it?'

'No, I got interrupted.'

'Well then, let's go back and have another look. After all,

where else do we go with him?'

'That was where I got attacked, though,' said Perry.

'There's two of us now. We can keep an eye. Keep a search going. Besides, Kirsten's out there,' said Ross.

'You know Kirsten well, don't you?'

'Kirsten joined us on the Isle of Lewis, looking into a murder at the cricket club. She was working as a uniformed constable at the time. Macleod was so impressed with her, she came and joined us in Inverness. She went off to the Service. Clever woman. He liked her a lot. But she was very like him.'

'She can certainly move. When I was struggling and she was taking on that other woman, she was quite something to watch. I mean, in all ways,' said Perry. He saw Ross staring back at him. 'Not that it would bother you.'

Perry started the car and drove back to the run-down estate, finding again the disused tenement building. Perry retraced his steps in through the rear door and up into the flat that had been Peter Green's.

'I searched through there and there was a secret hiding place in the back for photographs,' said Perry, pointing at the dresser in the living room.

'Well, he's got one, so he might have two,' said Ross. He went over to the window and looked outside.

'What are you doing?' asked Perry.

'Just checking. Keeping an eye that nobody's coming. Yeah?'

'Can you see anyone?'

'I can,' said Ross. 'There's a load of kids down there. Give me a minute.'

Ross disappeared down onto the street in front of the house. There were about eight kids there and Ross thought they should have been in school. A couple were on bikes and a few others were smoking. Ross approached them in his usual dapper suit.

'Are you lost, mate?' said one kid who must have been about fifteen.

'No,' said Ross. 'I want you to do a job for me.'

'A what? What do you think this is? Some sort of movie? Do a job for you?'

Ross realised he might have picked the wrong words. 'I want you to keep an eye on this building behind me. I'm inside it with a colleague. I don't want to be disturbed, if you understand.'

'I ain't doing nothing for nobody,' said one guy.

'You'll do it for money. I'll give you forty quid between you. I'm going to need about an hour.'

'Forty quid to do what?' said one boy.

'Want some of you at the front here so nobody goes in through that blocked up door. I want the other half of you around the back. The back door is open. I want you to sit in front of it, just play about in front of it, but if anybody comes to go in you holler.'

'Seriously?'

'Yeah,' said Ross. 'Can you do it?'

'Forty quid sitting on my bum? I'll do it,' said one of the lads who looked like he spoke for them all.

'Just be assured, if you don't do it, and you've taken my money, I'll come and get my money back. I'll take it back with interest.'

In some ways Ross wasn't comfortable with the way he was talking to the boys, but he didn't want them to think he was a policeman. He certainly would not pull out his warrant card. Then there would be explanations. Why are you looking in there? At the moment, the boys didn't know why. Ross took out the cash. 'There's twenty,' he said. 'When I come down, I'll give you another twenty.'

'Forty now,' said the boy, who looked like he was the leader.

'Don't want to be part of this? Twenty now, twenty after.' There were nods. Five minutes later, Ross was back up with Perry in the living room of Peter Green's flat.

'What did you do?' asked Perry.

'I've just got a bit of a guard up,' said Ross. 'Given what happened last time. I want to make sure we don't get any intruders.'

Perry searched round the skirting boards, seeing if they would come away. He put on evidence gloves again, once more for himself, because of the rat droppings around the edge of the carpet.

'Do you see anything that looks untoward? I mean, this furniture's not great, is it?'

'I'm no design guru,' said Perry. 'You're the fashion-conscious one with your snappy suits. You tell me if it doesn't look good.'

'You seen the bedroom yet?'

'Not been into it.'

Twenty minutes later, Perry and Ross were going through the bedroom. The large double bed, wardrobes, and the dressers that were still there. But Ross noticed a large cross on the wall. It was wooden and seemed to be fixed to the wall rather than hanging off anything. Ross put his hand on it.

'It's bizarre, isn't it?' said Perry. 'I wouldn't have thought he was religious.'

'I don't think he is. It's a good handle, this, though, isn't it?' said Ross. He grasped the cross and pulled at it. The section of the wall behind the cross came away with it, still attached, like some sort of child's toy where you had to fit the shape into the wall.

'Look at this,' said Ross, reaching inside.

He pulled out an envelope, opened it, and began putting photographs on the bed. There was Peter Green with lots of friends, or at least what looked like friends.

'A quiet life,' he said.

'One we don't know about,' Perry mused. 'Lots of people there. I don't recognise any of them. Barraclough's not amongst them.'

'No,' said Ross. 'But I recognise that club.'

'You do?'

'That's Glamour. It's not the sort of club you would go to. Specifically for the LGBTQ+ scene.'

'Oh, right,' said Perry. 'So he goes there, doesn't he?'

'I think that's the next port of call,' said Ross. 'We'll finish up, see if we can find anything more. But again, he's kept this secret. And it's obviously a big part of his life, if he's hiding it like this. After all, he hid the photographs of Barraclough too.'

It was about an hour later that Ross and Perry entered Glamour, Ross feeling himself forty pounds lighter. As they entered, they got questioning looks. But Perry noticed it was more at him than at Ross. *Was there some way that you knew?* Perry always wondered.

Perry had a thing where he thought he could tell where people were from. There were certain genetic factors that changed. He could never quite put them down, but he just knew when he looked at someone. Maybe it was like the computer in his head picking up different markers and saying, that's it. Perry wasn't totally sure how that worked.

But in this club, they seemed to identify Ross as being some-one that could, or should, be there, and Perry as someone who probably shouldn't. Maybe he was just being homophobic.

Ross approached one barman. He gave a smile. The club was quiet but then again, it was only in the afternoon.

'What can I do for you, love?' asked the barman.

'Good afternoon,' said Ross. 'I'm Detective Sergeant Alan Ross. This is Detective Constable Warren Perry. We're investigating someone who's been at your club. Peter Green? Looking to see if anybody knew him here. We believe he used to come to Glamour.'

'Okay,' said the barman. 'Not known to me by name. Do you have a photograph at all?'

Ross pulled out one photograph from the flat, showing Peter Green at the bar in Glamour with some friends standing beside him.

'Ah. I know the face. Can't say I knew him personally. That girl there in the photograph, that's Jenny. Lauren is Jenny's partner. Lauren's currently stacking drinks at the moment. She might tell you something about him.'

'Thank you,' said Ross, and allowed the man to direct him and Perry to Lauren. As they approached Lauren, Perry had to stop himself giving an audible gasp.

She turned round to face them, and although of average height, had shocking pink hair running down from the top of her head. She also had rings everywhere, studs in places that Perry almost shook at the idea of placing them into.

'Hello, Lauren,' said Ross. 'We're detectives. Detective Sergeant Alan Ross, DC Warren Perry. We'd like to ask you about Peter Green.'

'Peter? I know Peter. Is he okay?'

'When was the last time you saw him?'

'Oh, it's been months for Peter. Used to like to come down here. Was a quiet soul. Easily led, though. Lovely man. Would have done anything for you. Seemed a little afraid of something, though. He was happier here in the club. He struggled with coming out. Even in these latter days, when the world says it's all right, or encourages it.'

'So, you haven't seen him for a while?'

'It's been months,' she said. 'Peter was attracted to powerful men, and you could find a few of them in here. I've never seen him actually go off with anyone. But he liked to be about them.'

'I have some photographs of him at the club,' said Ross. 'Would you take a look for us?'

Lauren nodded. Her rings seemed to clink disturbingly to Perry as she approached the photographs, bracelets all the way down her arms. Perry thought half of her own weight must have been the jewellery she'd attached to herself. He was trying hard not to judge, but was finding it difficult to wrap his head around the woman's image.

'The people in the photo, it's the local crowd. They'll probably be here tonight, most of these people. Everybody except that one.'

She pointed in the photograph to a rather slender-looking man. He was certainly effeminate and had some very snappy clothing. The shirt was crisp, the trousers tight.

'You've never seen him?'

'I may have seen him but I don't remember him,' said Lauren. Ross went through the photographs but there was only one of the man and he was very close to Peter Green.

'And you say the rest of them are locals coming here for years?'

'We know our crowd.'

'Yes, we do,' said Ross.

The woman smiled back at him. 'I didn't mean that for you. I meant it for your friend.'

'So, the other guy,' said Perry, 'he's not local? Would you welcome him in?'

'I can't tell,' said Lauren. 'I don't remember him. I don't remember who he is. All I can tell you is, he's not here that often. Certainly rarely enough for me to forget him.'

'Thanks,' said Ross. He turned to Perry. 'I'll come back in here tonight. You rest up at the hotel. I'll see if anybody else knows him. I'll be able to fit in without looking too much like a sore thumb.'

Perry went to protest, but then stopped. He was on Ross's territory here, and he was the sergeant, after all.

'Are you sure, though? We don't want to split up.'

'I think I'll be all right here. Big crowd, plenty of people.'

Perry went off back to his hotel room. A package had arrived, and Perry took the box and placed it on the table within the room. He opened it up and lifted out many books.

'McGrubbin,' he said. 'They're saying McGrubbin, therefore I need to know what's in here.' He took one book, sat down on his bed, and opened it. He probably wouldn't hear from Ross until late that night. *Oh well*, thought Perry, *might as well get to work*. If he was lucky, the stories might be good.

Chapter 18

Hope sat in the car at Glasgow Airport, awaiting Susan Cunningham, who was routing in from Barra. It would be good to have Susan working alongside her again, for as much as she got on with Perry and Ross, there was something between her and Susan that seemed to click. Many people saw Susan as her protégé, very like her in looks, not quite the height, and certainly not the shocking red hair, but someone who was very similar.

Hope watched her emerge from the Glasgow terminal. No one could have guessed that she had lost her leg. For the woman walked confidently. The blonde-haired woman walked round to the rear of the car, opened the boot, flung her bag inside, before joining Hope in the front.

'Do you want me to drive?' asked Susan.

'It's fine,' said Hope. The team had an understanding that the junior partner would usually drive. Hope liked the privilege she had of sitting in the front seat during cases and contemplating instead of having to drive. She'd driven Macleod everywhere. But she thought she was a better driver than Macleod, anyway. Action wasn't always his middle name. Besides, she didn't want to think too much at the moment, for they were on their way to meet the family of David Funnell.

Local police had broken the news to the family that David was now dead. He had apparently gone on a business trip several days before—actually a week before—and the family hadn't heard from him. However, they thought the communications were bad. David had never left the country. Someone had grabbed him beforehand, before taking him to Colonsay to die.

The house that Hope pulled up to was in the west end of Glasgow, with a wall around it and a front door that led to four different flats. In saying that, they were big flats, and the overall building was quite colossal. In its day, there would have been a rich family staying there with plenty of servants. Nowadays, those sorts of houses were removed out to the country. The town equivalents were now four still quite considerable apartments.

Hope nodded at the policeman outside the front door and offered her warrant card. He gave a nod and explained that the family was upstairs along with a bereavement officer. Hope climbed the stairs up to the flat before ringing the doorbell and having it answered by that officer. Along with Susan, she entered a posh-looking hallway to be directed off into a living room.

A very large TV hung on the wall opposite a three-piece sofa that Hope could only dream of. It looked luxurious but the woman sitting in the middle of it—dabbing her eyes as she was held on to by what looked like a son and a daughter—told Hope that all riches didn't bring happiness.

'Thank you for seeing me,' said Hope, 'at this delicate time. I'm DI Hope McGrath. I'm investigating David's death. This is DC Susan Cunningham.'

'I'm Martina,' said the snivelling woman. She lifted her hand up to shake Hope's. 'This is my son and daughter.'

'I'm terribly sorry for your loss,' said Hope, 'but if you'll forgive me, I need to ask some questions.'

'Of course,' said the woman, but she clearly was struggling.

'Your husband was meant to be on a trip away; is that correct?'

'Yes, but he never called us from there. I was a little concerned, but, well, I thought little of it. He'd done that before. Sometimes he'd gone out on a ride to . . . well, you know what these trips can be. Sometimes they get taken off to places. Some places you wouldn't want to ring your wife from.'

Hope wasn't sure what these places would be. She'd never been on that sort of trip, but . . . She simply nodded.

'Did your husband have any connection with Colonsay?'

'No,' said Martina. 'I've no idea why he was up there.'

'Was he a reader at all?' asked Hope.

'Why?'

'He was found with a book.'

'Not that I'm aware of.'

'Your husband was for a long time a civic leader in Glasgow,' said Hope. 'Did he pick up many enemies during his time?'

'Well,' said Martina. 'Yes. David made a great stance against the crime lords in Glasgow. And over the years, he's suffered attacks—myself personally, even the children when they were at school. There was abuse, graffiti, sometimes threatening violence, but never any attempt at murder. It must be some criminal element looking to get their own back on him.'

'Have you had any threats recently?' asked Hope.

'None. None at all. He's retired now. I mean, why? Why

would you bother now? He's out of the picture.'

'He was around at the time of the McIntoshes, wasn't he?' asked Hope.

'They were one of the main families he went after, but it can't be them. There's nothing left of them. They were all broken up. David was happy about that. Very happy.'

'I could do with a list of his staff,' said Hope, 'those that worked with him. Even those in more recent times.'

'Hang on a minute.' Martina stood up and walked off out towards the kitchen. She'd came back in with a blonde-haired woman.

'This is David's old PA, Laura. She hasn't worked for him for a couple of years because he's been retired, but she'll have all the lists of people he worked with. She'll know them better than I will.'

'Excellent,' said Hope. 'Thank you very much. You don't mind if we look around?'

Martina shook her head, and the detectives spent the next twenty minutes examining the rooms. There were family photographs and, in every way, it looked like a happy family. There was nothing untoward and Hope felt bad having to do this search action amid such bereavement.

They soon left and, retiring to a coffee shop, they awaited the list of staff provided by his former PA. It didn't take long, and Hope and Susan began the journey to interview each of them. Coming towards teatime, Hope was feeling tired and Susan had taken over the driving. There weren't many left to visit, and so far, most of them had said the same thing. There had been threats made towards David, but they were very general, nothing specific.

Things had been sent in the post, but none of the interviewees had any personal experience of this. They arrived at the house of a Margaret Rosewood and knocked on the door of the semi-detached building. As they waited for it to be opened, a teen dressed in a school uniform rushed past them, opened the door, walked in and shut it behind them.

A few seconds later, the door was opened by a middle-aged woman.

'Sorry. Kids. I mean, they just don't think, do they? They just don't—'

'Would you be Margaret Rosewood?' asked Hope.

'Yes.'

'I'm DI Hope McGrath. This is DC Susan Cunningham. We'd like to ask you some questions about David Funnell.'

'David? It's been a long time since I worked for David. Well, a while. He's not in work anymore, is he?'

'No, he's not,' said Hope. 'I'm afraid to tell you that David actually is dead, and we're looking into his death.'

'Blimey,' said Margaret. She looked a little disturbed, as if she should say something, but wasn't sure if she should.

'Are you okay?' asked Susan.

'Yes. It's just . . . a bit . . . well, it's a bit of a shock, but . . .'

'But what?' asked Hope.

'You say you're looking into his death. Was it murder?'

'It certainly looks like it,' said Hope.

'I . . . well, maybe I shouldn't say this.'

'You shouldn't say what?' asked Hope.

'I left David's employ for a reason. I wasn't quite happy. He . . . well, he was quite shadowy and things.'

'How do you mean?' asked Hope.

The woman stepped outside the door, closing it behind her.

'My husband's in there. Now, understand we don't get on

particularly well, but we've kept going for the kids and that. So, please, what I'm about to tell you, you can't bring up in front of them.'

'Okay,' said Hope. 'I might need you to testify at some point.'

'I can't tell about this. But look, David, well David and I, we slept together for a while. He wanted me. I wanted some things from him. My life here wasn't going that well and it worked for me. I got some things from him, money and stuff, and a few other perks.

But I remember seeing him in hotels. We would be sleeping and then he'd say he'd have to get out of bed and go somewhere. Now most of these hotels were tiny budget places, converted houses, more like guest houses rather than full hotels. But I remember going and seeing where David was going because he was away with me. We were doing things on the sly. So that you would get out of bed and meet someone was, well, frankly, crazy.'

'Go on,' said Hope.

'Well, we would do what we were there to do and then I'd be sleeping and he'd get up in the middle of the night. He did this a few times, so I started following him. We were always in different guest houses but he would disappear into another room. I thought that was bizarre. Why do it? But he would talk to people. It was hard to hear what they were saying.'

'Did you recognise any of these people?' asked Hope.

'I never saw the people. But he always went off and was talking to them. And sometimes it was quite heated. I can't remember the conversations in full. Sometimes he would come back quite angry. Those weren't good times. Sometimes he took it out on me. Sometimes, he'd come back happy and then, well, he was waking me up for a different reason. I ended up realising that what I was getting out of him, from him, wasn't enough for the way he treated me. But I never made a fuss about it because, well, you didn't with David.'

'What do you mean?' asked Susan.

'I saw a few other girls who'd been ruined by him. Not around Glasgow anymore. Rumours spread about them because they were looking to blackmail David. He was a nasty piece of work. There's no way I'll stand up and say anything about him. But you should know. Maybe that'll help you. He was no angel. He talked about being this man who beat up the crime lords. I think he was as nasty as them behind it all.'

'I may need to come back and talk to you again,' said Hope. 'I won't say anything elsewhere, but if I come back to you, I may need to dig out some detail. We'll do it as discreetly as we can. I understand you wouldn't want to be out in public saying any of it.'

'Dear God, no,' said the woman. 'Best you can do for me is just forget that you heard it from me. But you need to know. You need to know.'

Hope thanked the woman and, together with Susan, returned to the car.

'So David Funnell is an upstanding citizen who seems to get heavily involved in stuff,' said Hope. 'Middle-of-the-morning rendezvous in houses is an excellent cover. Be away with the woman, so if anything happens, I'm having an affair.'

'What sort of a thing is an affair as good cover? What are you covering up if having an affair is okay and not the worst result?' asked Susan.

'Exactly,' said Hope, 'and he's determined to keep his good name as well. Obviously, he's got some sort of influence, if he's ruined people, but I wouldn't have thought he was on that level.

Are the people above him protecting him?' queried Hope.

'I don't know,' said Susan. 'It's hard to tell. Now, I think the family is genuinely sad.'

'Oh yes,' said Hope, 'but the presentation to us, daughter and son with the mother, the house, photographs, everything—it's all "this is a good family guy, a decent upstanding citizen." Yet there he is, having affairs, and the family would deal with it. Not him,—he's gone—the family, something behind him. She really did think it was the family when actually it was somebody else.'

'Anyway,' said Susan, 'I'm absolutely shattered. I think it's time to get back to the hotel. Same one as the boys?'

'Perry's booked rooms, so I hope so. It's a good idea to be closer together, anyway.'

'I'll message them, see if they want dinner,' said Susan.

Hope looked out the window back to the house that they'd just been to. This was often the problem when you were chasing people higher up the chain. Other people down the chain were afraid of them and didn't want to talk. You could throw down all your theories but you couldn't get it into a court, because you wouldn't have any witnesses.

'I can't believe that,' said Susan, staring at her phone.

'What?'

'Perry says Ross is off at some club and Perry's got too much work to get on with. He's not even coming for tea. You'd think it'd be better if we pulled together at this point,' said Susan.

She drove off in the car, Hope with a similar feeling. However, something was bugging her now. They had just been following a line of command here, being told where to go, being presented with the bodies and the surrounding detail. In the books and the places. She needed to get ahead of this because that's where they'd catch those who were doing it. Get ahead of them and win the game.

Chapter 19

Once again the morning sickness, or was it a nausea, had overcome her. Either way, it had driven Hope into the shower to try to feel more like herself. As she rinsed the suds off, her hand descended to her belly. It was definitely there—the bump. Her other hand came up and joined the first one. And for a moment she was just cradling this precious part at the front of her.

It wouldn't fall off. She was being daft now, but somewhere in there, someone was growing. Someone was coming alive. There was a little Hope. A little John. Maybe a mix of the pair of them. And part of her said 'Snap out of it. Get dried off, get back to work.' But there was a distinct part that said 'No.'

This will only come once. Certainly, only once with this child. Maybe she would have more, maybe not. Hope wanted to enjoy this. She'd been hauled away from John, was running around the country looking for people who were murdering. And yet this precious little life, this spark of opportunity, this unknown with so much potential, was growing away inside her.

Hope wasn't a deeply emotional woman. She was rational. But right now, she could feel tears beginning to flow. Not of sadness, but of joy. Or were they? In fact, she did not know why. But she was crying, holding on to her belly. It was another two minutes before she stopped.

She rinsed her face again underneath the shower's flow before switching it off and climbing out to get dried. When she'd done so, she walked into the main room and put on some pyjamas and wrapped a dressing gown around her. It was funny. She probably wouldn't have bothered with any of that at home if she'd been in her bedroom. But when she was on duty, she always felt she had to be prepared.

You never knew when somebody would knock on the door. You never knew when you got a phone call that suddenly became a video chat. And if you weren't wearing something appropriate, if you'd forgotten because you were just chilling out as yourself, well then. She had a rule there were no video chats in the house for she would have to check with John every time before she hit that button.

She laughed. It was probably more to do with the embarrassment of the people on the other end than any of her own. Hope sat down on the bed, pulled over her laptop, and brought up some details on the case. She checked the clock. Quarter past twelve. She should go to bed soon. After all, how much further was she going to get tonight?

There came a knock at the door. It was gentle, almost searching to see if she was awake. Well, it wasn't Ross. That would be quite firm. It wasn't Susan Cunningham. The sound would almost be excitable. And Susan wouldn't be bothering her unless it was something important. Hope swung her legs off the bed, walked over to the door, and peered through the peephole.

It was Perry. Of course, it was Perry. Only Perry could

knock delicately to check if you were up or not. She opened the door.

'Perry, what do I owe the pleasure at this time of night?' Perry was holding several books in his hand. 'What have you got there?' she said.

'I've been thinking,' said Perry, and he marched right past her into her room. He halted and turned. 'Sorry, I shouldn't have done that. Is it—?'

'It's fine, Perry. It's fine. I'm dressed. Not a problem. What?'

'Well, I . . . you said it was all about McGrubbin's books. The bodies all have McGrubbin's books. So, I read McGrubbin's books.'

'When did you read McGrubbin's books?'

'Earlier on today. Ross was going off to the nightclub. He said he'd be fine, so I thought, *I'll start reading these books because they seem to be important.* And they are. I tell you now, they are.'

'I did read them back in the day,' said Hope.

'Yes, but did you *read* them? I mean, did you *really read* them and see what's going on?'

'What do you mean?' asked Hope.

'*Two's a Squeeze.* That's book one, yes? Book one is *Two's a Squeeze.* It details—wait for this—an extra body buried in a grave to confuse the police. What did Macleod say? He said that Isbister was in another grave, in the same grave, two of them.'

'Okay,' said Hope. 'So somebody's written a story about it.'

'Yes, don't you see? They've written a story about the actual occurrence.'

'Yes,' said Hope, 'and they've matched it up. So, they found a book that says exactly what happened in that instance. So, they've used the book to direct us towards what's happened.'

'Book two. *The Gravedigger's Wife.*'

'That was, oh, something to do with multiple deaths.'

'How long ago did you read these?' said Perry. 'Book two is a book about a man used by others to murder over and over again. The man himself is addicted to power and dominates people. So, he's basically used. There's a whole psyche about him in it—how he can't get out of this cycle.'

'Okay,' said Hope.

'*The Gravedigger's Wife*. He's the wife. He's actually following the other man around. The man who's doing these killings. Don't you see?'

'So, they've used the book again to show us who Peter Green was,' said Hope.

Perry shook his head. 'The other book. *A Hand on the Tiller,*' said Perry. 'You read that one?'

'Yes, I've read it. I read it ages ago. It's another crime one. It's about a guy who's stuck in the middle.'

'A guy who is stuck in the middle. Who's controlling the groups who murder. Who gets instructions from above. Somebody who's had—'

Hope gasped. 'Hang on. What are you suggesting?'

'Wait for it,' said Perry. 'Have you read the book *Selector* by McGrubbin?'

'*Selector*. That's about somebody marking out hits or something, isn't it?'

'It's a man who picks a target to kill and gets others to do it.'

'So,' said Hope, 'what are you saying—that our next one is going to be this victim, this man who picked the targets; that's going to be the next victim?'

'That's one side of it,' said Perry. 'In the book *Selector*, the man is snappily dressed. Really snappily dressed. He's effeminate as well. Peter Green was in a photograph with a snappily dressed man. That man was not a regular at the nightclub that Peter Green went to. He's not a close friend.'

'But you're saying—'

'How do you write this?' asked Perry. 'Why does this come in so accurately? You said the books were "roughly about" but the books are not roughly about anything. The books are direct stories about who these people are. Yes, the names have changed. But my goodness, there's some other, well, possibly other fictitious deaths and stuff in it. But these are our victims. These books are based on these people.'

'That's a bit of a stretch, Perry, isn't it? How can you do that? Are you saying that she wrote—J.F. McGrubbin wrote—these, and then somebody looked at them and then copied the books? We've had that before, though. You know that. We had that film that came out, and everybody was getting killed in the same way as the film. But that was a lunatic. We're talking about organised—'

'We're talking about an organised group of people doing this. Organised very similar to the way the people in the books are organised. And there's a detailed study on each of them. These books are not trashy police procedural things. These books are detailed studies on the people around the author.'

'What did Macleod say?' asked Perry. 'Macleod said that there was a group of people above. And there's a group of people who are pushing us on. So, the ones above don't want us to find out. Not the people up above. Well, as we go higher and higher, we're going to find out as the layers are more and more removed. We're getting shown the plods right now, the people at the bottom. Gradually, we're working up. Who would know about these people? Who could write them in such detail?'

'Those who were above, those who were reaching down to control them,' said Hope.

'Exactly, and McGrubbin has got all these people and has written about them, because who in their right mind is going to accuse her of actually basing it on real life? And their stories are different, so the books don't follow on to each other but they're talking about different people within an organisation. Our victims are being presented. She's a writer, she's writing what she knows, she's writing what she's seen.'

Hope sat down for a moment. 'That's a stretch, Perry. That's a real stretch.'

'And yet, how else do you explain this? How do you explain these books turning up in the right place? They are aimed towards McGrubbin. People doing this are telling us that McGrubbin's in on it.'

'Look, Perry,' said Hope. 'Are you sure? You said you'd just started. How did you get through four books already?'

'Five. I'm still working on the rest of them. I speed read. I've trained myself to speed read when I have to.'

'But to come up with it all—'

'I'm not the action man in our team. I'm not the person who digs out numbers and files and traces transactions and journeys. This is why I'm here,' said Perry. 'Trust me, this is too much of a coincidence. You bring Ross in here, he's going to ask you where's my evidence. All I've got are stories that look like they match, fictional stories that look like they possibly match up to characters. But we also have these books being placed inside the bodies. Victims who are not random. They were executed, remember?' said Perry. 'These are not random people. Specifically chosen people, books specifically chosen to go with them.'

'Do you think McGrubbin's somewhere in this group? McGrubbin is—'

'I think McGrubbin's got to be a target,' said Perry. 'Got to be. You wouldn't know everybody. Think about it. Barraclough and Peter Green, they probably know David Funnell. But the person above David Funnell, Barraclough and Green aren't going to know them, are they?'

'Well, Green's in a photograph with them.'

'Green's in a photograph with a man who we haven't been told is a friend of his. In fact, he's not a friend of his. He's been identified as being an obscure person there.'

Hope walked over to the window, pulled back the curtains and stared out into the Glasgow night.

'Perry,' she said, and heard Perry walk over towards her. 'I think, well, I have to say—' She turned and saw Perry's expectant face and rushed right past him towards the bathroom. She slammed the door behind her, got down on her knees, opened up the lid of the toilet and grabbed her hair quickly before she vomited.

'Are you okay?' asked Perry. 'Do you need some help? Do you need—'

'Fine, Perry,' said Hope. She almost spat into the bowl. 'It's just sickness. It's just the baby. I'm fine. Give me a minute.'

It was five minutes later when Hope came back out of the bathroom. Her face was drenched with sweat and she was extremely pale. She could see the eyes of concern on Perry.

'I'm fine,' she said. 'I think you might be on to something. But it's a stretch. But it's a stretch we need to look into. I think we need to go find our author. Sooner rather than later. Check out a few more of those books. She wrote a lot, McGrubbin.'

'She did,' said Perry. 'And I've been lucky so far. Well, I've read the ones that we know are involved. I don't know about the others. But I'll get on it.'

'Well done, Perry,' said Hope. She walked to the door. 'Don't worry about me. I'm fine.'

'Are you sure? Do you want me to get Susan to come to you? Susan could sit with you. I understand you might be bothered about having me help you. But Susan's a woman. Susan could help you. Susan could—'

'Perry, go read those books,' said Hope. She shut the door on him, took one breath, and then another. *He was a decent man, but my goodness, he is overpowering. Right,* thought Hope. *What do I do now?* And then she turned and ran back to the bathroom, the decision taken out of her hands.

Chapter 20

Dominic reached down and pulled up his hiking socks. He was feeling a little sore, but he'd been on the move for the last three weeks. Today, he was on Rum, having taken the ferry over. Rum was not large and it was quiet, offering an opportunity to get away from it all. He had, as per usual, come looking for something specific.

Dominic found if he didn't plan to see something, he just wandered and really got nowhere. Instead, he was looking for the mausoleum of the Bullough family. It wasn't a particularly exciting destination, but it was a destination, and you always had to have a destination. If you didn't, you were just lost.

Dominic wasn't lost. He was experiencing life, living after a big city job. A job that nearly destroyed him. Dominic wanted adventures. And so, he'd come away, up to Scotland, and off to the more remote parts.

Rum and Eigg were remote. Small islands with not a lot of people. And on this clear, crisp day, he was enjoying himself, getting to see something that other people wouldn't. What he would do, when he got to the mausoleum, was take plenty of photographs. He'd upload it to his podcast. And he'd maybe post something on his YouTube channel.

So far, he was a bit disappointed that only twenty-three people seemed to be invested in his journey on the channel. His journey away from being an office-dominated worker, somebody who was a slave to the grind, to now being this free spirit.

He stood up and breathed in the air—so much fresher than in London. He looked down at his phone, which was showing a compass at this time, with a map in the corner. Rum wasn't the most difficult to navigate, and he wandered on, confident he was going in the right direction for the mausoleum. He wasn't too sure about the history of the Bullough family or why they had a mausoleum. But it was somewhere to go, something to photograph when he was there, and something to tell everyone about. Because everyone would need to know, even if they didn't know it yet.

The YouTube channel would grow, and maybe one day he would monetise it. Maybe one day he would be big enough that people would talk about him. It would come, he was assured of it.

The mausoleum was close to the coastline. Not that anywhere in Rum was far from the coast, being the small island that it was. The mausoleum, when he saw it, was a grey stone affair, certainly worth a photograph or two. Thankfully, the sun was shining, and the waters behind it would be a terrific backdrop.

Dominic entered quickly to see what else would be inside that he could photograph. And then reared up slightly. There was someone lying on the floor. Why were they lying on the floor here? Surely you didn't get homeless people on Rum? Why would you get a homeless person here? It was the back end of nowhere, wasn't it? There weren't that many people who lived on Rum. They would have their own houses. They wouldn't be sleeping in mausoleums.

He walked forward a few more steps, looking down at the man. There was blood at the side of him.

Really? thought Dominic. *You had an accident?*

This would be quite interesting. Dominic's heart thumped. Imagine getting a photograph of this up on his website? Or on his podcast, detailing it, how he'd found somebody who'd injured themselves.

He looked down at the man's clothing. They were pretty fine threads. He'd seen that sort of style and suit. Certainly they were expensive. And those shoes, those shoes were worth at least two hundred.

Kneeling down, he followed the man's legs up to the torso and then got to the face. *Oh*, he thought, *quite a girlish look about him.* And then Dominic's eyes dropped and he saw where the blood had come from. The man's neck was cut open.

Most people would have reared away but Dominic pulled out the phone and began to video the deceased. He stood up over him before walking back to the entrance.

'So, everyone,' he said to his now recording phone. 'I've arrived at Bullough Family Mausoleum, and I've found this. A dead body. I'm actually stuck with a dead body on the Isle of Rum. Isn't that exciting? Now, obviously, I need to call this in to the police. I think the man's definitely dead. He's not moving at all. But let's see if I can record my phone call, so you can see it happening in real time.'

Dominic checked his phone and realised that the mobile signal wasn't there. He'd had a signal when he came to Rum. Maybe he just needed to be in a different part of the isle. That was a pain, wasn't it? Fortunately, Dominic had two phones, and pulling out the second one, he marched out of the mausoleum, back along his path until he restored the signal on the phone. He then set the first one up to record him being on the second phone.

It took a couple of minutes for the phone call to be placed and for Dominic to give coordinates before he made his way back inside.

It would be a good while before the police got there, so Dominic decided to do a little filming before they arrived. He got back down beside the body, bringing up his camera close, filming himself the whole time, and then stopped for a second. There was something inside the deceased's waistcoat. He reached down and unbuttoned it. And there, lying on the man's chest, inside a zippy bag, was a book.

'*Selector*,' he said. 'Wow. McGrubbin.' He picked up the book, opened it, and started flicking through the pages. He then turned and put the camera on himself, detailing to his listeners how he had found this body, and how the book was inside the man's clothing. Dominic went outside and filmed himself approaching, and then inside and out, and made detailed studies with the camera of where the body was.

He narrated about how the body would have been brought in, and where the body was possibly killed. Only when he heard the helicopter coming did it stop him in his filming frenzy.

What are they doing with that helicopter? It just drowns the sound out. It's going to be—he ran outside and saw it was a police helicopter. Dominic, not put off in the slightest, picked his phone up again and began to film the helicopter as it landed on Rum.

* * *

The call had come in advising of a body on Rum, and Ross had taken it directly to Hope. They made for the airport, Ross and Jona, Jona only having just arrived in Glasgow from Colonsay.

Macleod had organised a police helicopter. Given how thin the teams were spread, Jona had wanted to get there to preserve the scene of the crime as soon as she could. Rum was a funny place in the sense that it was off the beaten track. There weren't that many people there, so if she could get there quickly, she could probably stop any contamination. So far, the killers had been good, and had prevented themselves from leaving anything behind that would incriminate them, but Jona never gave up.

Ross had been free at the time. After a quick discussion with Hope—she said she was going to talk to J.F. McGrubbin, and she wanted Perry to remain working on the books—it was decided that Ross and Jona should go as a pair up to Rum. Susan Cunningham would remain to assist Hope.

Ross had heard a load of mumbo-jumbo from Perry, talking about what was in his mind, books and that. At the end of the day, it was scenes of crime that mattered. It was solid evidence. He struggled with Perry, for the man came up with so many theories, and from doing what? Sitting back and just listening. Now from reading books, which was a stretch, to say the least.

The helicopter ride up to Rum gave Ross the chance to get some glorious scenery. Using his camera, he took some photographs but as they routed in towards Rum, he became more serious minded.

They could see a figure waving at them from beside the mausoleum, where the body was reported to be. Ross wasn't familiar with the Bullough family and their mausoleum. Running through his mind was to check the different names in the area. He'd also scanned the sea and couldn't see a motorboat. Now, as they touched down, the man who'd been waving was back inside the mausoleum. He saw Jona, her eyes livid with rage. What was the man doing in there?

The doors of the helicopter were slid back, seatbelts unclipped, and Ross and Jona ran over towards the mausoleum. Jona was quicker than Ross and tore into the mausoleum first, and Ross heard her cry out to the man who was inside.

'Step back from the body, sir. Sir, step back!'

'He had this book on him. It was inside his waistcoat. I've taken it out! I've started to read some of it. It's a book by an author, called—'

'Put the book down. Step away from the body, please.'

Ross stepped up beside Jona. He could see why she was livid. The body looked as if it had been moved. The book that normally was with these bodies was now in the man's hands, a zippy bag abandoned on the floor.

'I do not believe this,' said Jona under her breath.

'Sir,' said Ross, 'step back. Step back, please.'

'Oh, it's all right. He's dead,' said the man.

'You're in the middle of a crime scene. You are contaminating that crime scene,' pleaded Jona. 'Sir, you are changing everything from the way it was when you came in. Step away, please.'

'I'm not squeamish. It's not a problem. I've just been videoing some of it for my YouTube channel.'

'You've done what?' blurted Ross.

'My YouTube channel. I used to be a banker in the city.'

Ross stared at the man incredulously. 'I'm not going to say

it again. You need to put the book down and you need to step over here with me.' The man looked at Ross, disappointed but he put the book down, and started to walk across.

'Not there!' shouted Jona. Ross could see the problem. The man walked through the blood on the floor as he came over to Ross.

'Are you Dominic?' asked Ross.

'Yes, I'm Dominic. Pleased to meet you,' said the man. He reached out to shake Ross's hand. Ross was quick enough to spot the blood on his hand.

'I need you to step outside with me, sir. Jona, are you okay?'

Ross said this hopefully. Jona, however, looked as if she was apoplectic. If she had been a rocket on fireworks night, she couldn't have been more ready to explode up in the sky.

'I will be,' said Jona quietly.

Ross indicated for the man to go outside and told him to sit down on a nearby rock.

'OK, sir, I need your phone.'

'My phone?'

'Yes, sir. You said that you took images. You said that you were making video for your YouTube channel. I need to see all of it now. I'm afraid I'll have to take your phone off you.'

'It's OK. I phoned it in. I mean, I didn't do this. You are aware I didn't do this. No killer in their right mind would kill somebody and then stand there making a YouTube documentary on it, would they?'

No, thought Ross, *they wouldn't. But neither would anybody else finding a dead body start to make a YouTube documentary about it when they had just called the police.* He took a deep breath. *Other people had the decency to scream, be distressed and run off. That was normal. Got them out of the crime scene quickly.*

'You can't take my phone, anyway. I need the phone. That's the only copy I've got of the footage.'

'The footage, sir, that you will *not* be putting onto a channel. Have you streamed it up yet?'

'No, no. I always take it home first. I always prep it, put it through the video editor. You've got to be sure you get the colours. I've got a cracking shot of the man's neck where it's cut fully open. That's quite something, isn't it? Do many people die that way?'

Ross took a deep breath. He had a feeling this was going to be a long one. 'Put your phones out in front of you, sir.' The man did so and Ross took out a zippy bag from inside his own pockets, placing the phones inside and then inside his own jacket.

'I suggest you wait here a moment, sir. I need to make a phone call.'

Ross put a phone call in to Hope, advising of the situation, and Hope told him to get hold of the coastguard. Ross was to get an idea from Jona how long the man had been dead and then find out how far a motorboat could go in that time. It would help the search. Ross, unwilling to leave Dominic on his own, went to the entrance of the mausoleum and shouted in for Jona.

'Give me an idea how long he's been dead,' asked Ross.

'Which one—the body inside the mausoleum or the guy sitting over there on the rock I'm about to kill?'

'Mausoleum. I need it as good as you can. It's going to help with the search.'

'He isn't dead over three hours,' said Jona.

Ross called the coastguard, advised the timings, and asked them to plot how far a motorboat could get away. They were then to advise the search coordinators, who were already looking for the boat.

Once he'd done that, he walked back over to Dominic. The man was still grinning like a Cheshire cat.

'OK,' said Ross. 'We're going to take this from the top. Everything you've done today. How you found the body. What you did afterwards. And we're going to go through it at least twice.'

'Do you mind if I record this for my channel?' said Dominic.

If Jona doesn't kill him first, thought Ross, *I may just do it myself.*

Chapter 21

With Ross up in Rum, Hope continued her search for McGrubbin. She called her agent and was given the address of a house in Mallaig, along with a phone number and mobile. However, her agent said that McGrubbin was a quiet person and often wouldn't take calls from any number she didn't know. On putting the theory to the test, Hope found her calls went unanswered.

'I'm not happy about it,' said Hope. 'If we have a theory running that McGrubbin could be involved in this—that the books could be about real people, or at least caricatures of them—she might be next on the list.'

'The house is up in Mallaig,' said Perry. 'It's not that far up the coast. We should head out.'

'I agree,' said Susan Cunningham.

'Well, the only other line of attack,' said Hope, 'is that something comes in on the boat, the *Alecto*. Susan, can you get over to where the search is being based out of? Have a word with them, see what's coming from it. Perry and I will spin over to Mallaig, see if McGrubbin's in. You can join us later, if need be.'

'I thought we weren't splitting up,' said Susan.

'You'll be fine. You're off to one of our places, not out and about searching. Ross should come back down at some point. You can join up with him to head about after that.'

Susan clearly wasn't happy about being taken out of the action. But it was Perry who had come up with this idea that McGrubbin could be involved. Hope wanted him with her in case it came to questions. Perry could often get round the other side of people, see through any screens they were throwing up in front of you.

The drive up to Mallaig allowed Hope time to relax. That morning had been another one of running to the bathroom and the effects were showing on her. She thought her eyes looked a little bleary, to say the least.

But, as some women often find, their hair became an unnatural thing of beauty during pregnancy, and Hope's red strands were shining even more than normal. There was a gloss to it that even Perry had commented on, though delicately. He was learning to tread carefully in the land of the pregnant woman.

It was late morning when they arrived in Mallaig, and Perry pulled up at a house on the outskirts. It wasn't quite a mansion, but more of a dainty cottage. There was a car in the driveway, a little sporty number, that made Hope think of Clarissa's little green car. She hoped McGrubbin wasn't of the same ilk as Clarissa; otherwise, it could be an interesting conversation.

Hope pulled her leather jacket on and walked up to the front door of the house. She pressed the doorbell, which rang, but then noticed that the door itself wasn't fully closed. Perry joined her and spotted it straight away.

'Hey, that door's open,' he said. He rapped the door and shouted inside, but got no response. 'Shall we?' he asked.

Hope pushed the door open and stepped into a rather sumptuous hallway. As she walked along it, she could see pictures of book fairs, signings. Certainly, McGrubbin had no problems with being a centre of attention.

'Miss McGrubbin?' shouted Perry. 'I'll go upstairs,' he said to Hope.

'Together,' she replied. 'Remember what Seoras said.'

She turned and followed Perry up the stairs, then to a far part of the cottage. They searched through two bedrooms. One had been slept in. The other was clearly for visitors. There was a delicately styled kitchen, wooden effect timber on the ceiling. But there was no author. McGrubbin was not here.

'Today's meal,' said Perry, looking at the half-eaten plate of food in the lounge.

'Maybe she's popped out for a walk,' said Hope.

'We're not that lucky,' said Perry.

'Well, let's talk to the neighbour.'

They stepped outside, walked down the drive, and to the next cottage along, which was some hundred yards away. Rapping the front door, a woman shouted from the rear before emerging with rubber-gloved hands and a sponge in her hand.

'Cleaning the floor,' she said, seeing Perry look at her. The woman was short, her hair tied up behind her, and wore an apron.

'Sorry to bother you,' said Hope. 'I'm DI Hope McGrath. This is DC Warren Perry. We're looking for Miss McGrubbin next door.'

'She should be there,' said the woman, and then looked past Hope. 'Yes, the car's there. No reason she shouldn't be there. She didn't say she was going anywhere.'

'Do you talk frequently?' asked Perry.

'Talked this morning. She normally comes out for a stroll early on, and if I see her, I say hello, as you do. And she had nothing planned today. I thought she was writing. She's got a wee office in that cottage where she writes. Doesn't normally go out to do it.'

'Thank you,' said Hope, and the pair returned to McGrubbin's cottage.

'So, what do we do?' asked Perry.

'If she's gone out for the messages, shopping or whatever, or she's just gone for a walk, she'll be back. Nothing to worry about. If somebody's taken her, we need to move,' said Hope.

'Well, if they've taken her, they'll be heading for the boat, assuming my theory's right, about her being involved in this.'

'Mallaig Harbour,' said Hope. The pair jumped in the car before racing off. It was only a five-minute drive to Mallaig Harbour and when they arrived, Hope spotted a uniformed police officer walking along the pier. She strode over to him with Perry.

'Officer, DI McGrath. Have you been canvassing around here for the boats?'

'Yes,' he said. 'As per instruction, we've been making a note of who's in each and every day.'

'Have you seen an *Alecto*? A motor launch? *Alecto*?'

'No *Alecto*,' said the man. 'Not seen anything of that. That was in the brief, to look for that one. Nothing on that front.'

'What else has happened?'

'This is Mallaig, isn't it? We get a fair bit of traffic in and out. Nothing too busy. Lifeboat went out earlier. A routine job, I heard. Some of the fishing boats have come in and out. It's not really the time of year for many motor launches. There was one earlier, though.'

'Do you have it on your list of who was here?' asked Perry.

'I have just finished typing it up on the laptop in the car. Come with me,' said the man.

Hope watched as Perry disappeared off with the officer. She turned and stared out at the water. If they got McGrubbin away now, it'd be too late. Where would she turn up? Where was there called after the author? What book would she be killed with? She didn't enjoy having to get ahead, having to work out the clues to be presented. Anyway, other than the location, knowing the book didn't help. She turned and walked over towards the police car where the officer was opening up his laptop for Perry.

'You see here, Warren,' the officer said to Perry, 'that's the list from today. New one came in. I was here this morning. Motor launch.'

'*Megaera*,' said Perry.

'Yes,' said the man. 'Funny spelling. I don't know how you write that one down properly.'

'What have you got, Perry?' asked Hope from the other side of the car.

'*Megaera*. It's one of the Furies. Like Alecto.'

Hope was stunned by Perry's knowledge. As soon as he had a slight detail, he seemed to read all around it. Definitely a different sort of digging to Ross.

'They're not going to just sit and leave the same name on the boat, are they?' continued Perry. 'Too easy to spot. And yet they still want to advertise what they're doing. Who they are. When did that vessel go?' asked Perry to the officer.

'Well, I'm back here, what, twenty minutes? Thirty minutes? So it's gone sometime between then and previously. I was there about two hours before.'

'Timing's right,' said Hope. 'The timing's right. Talk to me about the motorboat. Tell me about it.'

'Couple of guys. A woman, I think,' said the officer.

'What did the woman look like?'

Perry picked out his phone and gave Hope a nod. 'It's okay, I've got it.' He produced a photograph of McGrubbin on his phone and placed it in front of the officer. 'Did you see this woman?'

'Miss McGrubbin? No. No, she wasn't here.'

Perry let go a sigh of relief. But Hope wasn't so easily distracted. 'Tell me what they did,' she said.

'They went ashore. They said to me they were going to get supplies. That's quite common. You know, we've got a supermarket here. And then they said they'd be going out again.'

'Out to do what?' asked Hope.

'Fishing. They said they were going fishing. It looked like you could put fishing rods on the back with one of those chairs. You know, they sit in and fish off the back, but I didn't think that was the way they did it here. But rich people with money, they come up here and just hire this stuff. They haven't a clue what they're doing,' said the officer.

'Strange time of year to be doing it, though,' said Perry.

'Oh, that's true, most of them are here closer to summer. They don't like our cold weather. Hot enough for them in the summer.'

'Anything else about the boat?' asked Hope.

'I don't think so. There's a harbour master down there in the office. You can ask them. They might have some detail on it.'

Perry thanked the man, told him to keep on doing what he

was doing with recording the vessels. Hope and Perry strode down to the harbour master's office, knocking on the small door.

'Come in.'

Inside, an older man was sitting back in his seat, staring at a computer.

'Can I help you?' he asked.

Hope pulled out a warrant card. 'DI Hope McGrath, this is DC Warren Perry. We're looking for some details on a vessel.'

'Oh, we got your thing. Yes, we've been keeping a lookout for *Alecto*. Not come through here. Have heard nothing about it. Spoken to some of the other harbour masters and they know nothing either.'

'Do you know a *Megaera*?' asked Hope.

'Yes, it was in here this morning. Motor launch but has since disappeared off. Came in for some supplies and also to pick up a package.'

'A package? What sort of package? Like post?'

'No, not the post office. There was a crate arrived.'

'What sort of size of crate?' asked Perry.

'Well, it was smallish. Quite low down. Narrow case. Something that looked like it would have a rod in it, or several rods in it.'

'The length of it, what would you say?' asked Perry.

'Six feet long, maybe. Oh, two feet wide, be a touch less. Again, maybe two feet up.'

'And did you see inside the crate?' asked Perry.

'Didn't touch it. Not my business. When it arrived, I told the guy who brought it just to leave it down, although it seemed quite a struggle for him. Had a couple of handles on it. I asked if I should give him a hand. He said he was fine but he didn't look it. But he put it down beside where *Megaera* was because they'd gone off, anyway. I went back about my duties, and when *Megaera* was departing, the crate was gone. They'd taken it on board.'

Hope looked over at Perry, but the man was deep in thought.

'Well, thank you,' said Hope. She stepped outside of the office. Perry was slow to follow but when he did, he only took a step outside, and then stopped, looking at the water.

'What's the matter?' asked Hope.

'Hope, we've got *Megaera*, so maybe we should start looking for it.'

'Yes, could be something.'

'It is something,' said Perry. 'Six feet long, two feet wide, two feet up. You could store a person in there.'

'Store a person?'

'No fuss, nothing unusual about it, is there,' said Perry. 'Somebody delivers a crate, looks like a load of rods inside. But the guy insists on carrying them himself because it will be heavy, heavier than what rods would be. You don't get questions, not if somebody else is doing it.'

'You think that's her going onto that boat?'

'We need to get some units in the air, to get people out in the water. We need to find that boat,' said Perry. 'If my theory's right, McGrubbin's next, it's just a case of where they're taking her.'

'That could be anywhere. We don't get told until afterwards, don't get the clues in advance. We've never been ahead in this.'

'Then we need to,' said Perry. 'Do you know what? I might just have an idea.'

Chapter 22

Hope was occupied on the phone, calling Susan Cunningham and advising her where the search should now be looking. She wanted helicopters. She wanted anything she could get in the air. The coastguard had planes, didn't they, for searching? They needed to find this vessel. It was now becoming a race against time.

She was standing a little off the car that Perry and she had arrived in, and Hope was focusing out on the water. Perry, by contrast, had gone to the boot of the car, into some of his gear, and pulled out some books. He jumped into the back seat of the car, put some books on the seat, and flicked through them.

'Have you got a moment when you're ready?' Hope shouted at Perry.

The man put his hand up in a stopping motion, showing he shouldn't be disturbed. *What is he doing? He is the constable. I'm the inspector. He needs to get himself out here to help me.*

But what did he need to help her with? Susan had taken down the detail. Susan was chasing things up. Hope thought she should talk to Macleod. He could pull some strings, maybe even get Jim on board. It was just easier acquiring assets with Jim on board sometimes. She called Macleod.

'It's Hope. I think our author, McGrubbin, has been taken.'

'What do you mean?'

'Perry's got this crazy idea and he just might be right. In the books of McGrubbin, the central figures within them appear to be about those who have died. Perry got the idea that McGrubbin actually knows what's going on. McGrubbin's part of this. And she used these characters in her book. Now, she's written loads of books, so it's very specific books she's used them in. It's not like she's just written a series all about this. These are very specific books within a larger context.'

'And so why do you think she is involved?' asked Macleod.

'Because she must have known these people to write about them. Therefore, Perry's assumption is she's higher up the chain. And she's accidentally, or unwittingly, or maybe even deliberately put some of it down in her books. She's made the characters. She's used them. But of course, nobody's going to know them all except the person at the top. The ones at the bottom won't know the ones two up from them, if it's just some sort of secret society.'

'And you say she's missing,' said Macleod.

'We went to her house today. Front door open. Not locked. No alarms. We have a boat, *Megaera*.'

'You mean *Alecto*,' said Macleod, and then he stopped. '*Megaera*?'

'It's one of the other Furies,' said Hope. 'They probably changed the name. It's a motorboat that came to Mallaig, where McGrubbin lives. A box was delivered to it today, and the box could easily hold a person. In fact, it would be perfect for someone who was knocked out and laid down.'

'Okay,' said Macleod. 'So, what do you want from me?'

'Get hold of Jim. I need air assets, I need stuff that can search the waters here, in a fast way. I need to find this boat, it'll be off somewhere—.'

'Somewhere to kill her, like the ones before? How long's it been gone?'

'It could have a two-hour jump on us, nearly. An hour and a half, two hours.'

'And it's a motorboat,' said Macleod. 'That's quite a bit of distance. A lot of water to cover.'

'It is,' said Hope. 'Perry thinks he can get ahead of it, though. Perry's going to try to work out where they're going.'

'How?' asked Macleod. And Hope stopped. Perry was going to do it by reading books, but she wasn't sure how.

'Perry, come here a minute.' The man slowly clambered out of the car, holding a book in his hand. Hope pressed the speaker on the phone.

'Seoras is on. He wants to know how you're going to work out where they're going.'

'Everything's been in the books, Seoras. All the characters have been in the books. Now, the people who are doing it realise this, and that's the way they're giving us the clue. McGrubbin must be in the book. What her other role is must be in the book. Not an author, but that other person. She's actually vain enough to have written about this. This is her waving it in the face of everyone. Successful author, doing what she's doing without anyone knowing.'

'How many books has she got?' asked Macleod.

'Seventy-odd?' said Perry. 'But I'm narrowing it down. I know the type of book, know the type of cover she's got on it. I'm searching through some at the moment.'

'How are you going to read all those books?' asked Macleod.

'With a little bit of peace and quiet,' said Perry. Hope saw him look up at her. His face almost panicking, he'd said too much.

'Fine,' said Macleod. 'Get on it.' Hope shrugged her shoulders as she saw Perry become highly relieved.

'You heard him,' said Hope. 'Get to it.'

'I'll go talk to Jim. See what we can do to help you. Okay. Where are you going from here?' asked Macleod.

'I'm in Mallaig. Last place *Megaera* was seen. No point going anywhere else. I don't know where to go.'

'Okay, it'll just be a search, then. It'll be a hunt unless Perry comes up with something.'

Hope spent the afternoon back and forward with Susan Cunningham. There were a couple of what they thought were sightings, but it was the wrong boat when people got close. The Coastguard had provided an aircraft which trailed up and down the waters on the west coast of Scotland, reporting in every now and again on certain boats. So far, the launch hadn't been seen. Maybe it was being hidden at the moment.

Time was ticking, and Hope could feel the pressure. What didn't help was that halfway through the afternoon, the nausea struck again, and she had to run to be sick several times. She managed to stop Perry, however, trying to mollycoddle her, telling him to get back to his books.

As the light was going in the early evening, she saw Perry get out of the car, holding a book in front of him.

'This one,' he said. 'This novel.'

'What novel?' asked Hope.

'*The Hand of God*. This woman. You should read this. The arrogance!'

'Calm down, Perry. What?' said Hope. 'What have you got?'

'The story is about someone who picks out the targets, runs

a group which goes about avenging wrongs. They step in and they take out people who are untouchable, too strong, too powerful,' said Perry. 'However, there are lots and lots of locations where things happen. But what she does do, this person, is organise a lot of the leaders being brought to a specific island where they have a sacrificial site. This book talks more and more about how it's a cause. It's almost a religious activity, capturing the wrong-doers, bringing them back. It's quite scary,' said Perry.

'But where's the site? Where is this sacrificial site?'

'It's what they call the Big Island in the book. They refer to it as Big Island.'

Hope put her hands to her head. She felt the nausea again. But this was more than that. They were there. They were right there. And she couldn't get what it was.

'Big Island. What does that mean? Where do we get Big Island from? There's nowhere in Scotland called Big Island, is there?'

'It's also Holy Ground, though. It's described as Holy Ground,' said Perry.

'We got a Holy Ground? We've got a Holy Island, haven't we?'

'That's what I've got, okay? I'll keep reading,' said Perry. 'But this ties in. They use a knife in this. They cut them through the throat from behind. Jona said sacrificial. Jona said it looked like a ritual. This book's got a ritual in it. It's the one!'

Hope called Macleod, hoping at least she could churn over what Perry had said with him. He might have some ideas. After all, that's what he was good at.

'Macleod.'

'Perry reckons it's in the book, *Hand of God*," Seoras. And he says in the book, there's a character who basically controls all of this, all these killings. So, he's surmising McGrubbin is this person. He says the arrogance is in the writing. He can hear it, he can—'

'Does it have a place?' asked Macleod.

'The book only describes it as Big Island in the book.'

'Big Island?'

'Yeah, Big Island. We haven't got anywhere called Big Island, have we?' she said.

'Eilean Mòr,' said Macleod. 'Gaelic, Scots Gaelic, Eilean Mòr.'

'What?' said Hope.

'It's my language. Lewis, we speak Scots Gaelic, remember? Eilean Mòr. Lots and lots of the West Coast is named in Scots Gaelic.'

'So all we've got to do is find Eilean Mòr.'

'Eilean Mòr's everywhere,' said Macleod. 'Big island. You know, it's not difficult. It's like Newtown. Newton, you know. Every town was new. They called it Newton something. Newton this, Newton that. Big island. Eilean Mòr.'

'But it's got to be a big one, hasn't it? I mean, I guess it's a significant island, isn't it?'

'No,' said Macleod. 'There're loads of them. There are many islands. Little spaces. Little spots. In Glasgow, at one point, I had to catalogue a lot of these islands.'

'Why?'

'Well, it wasn't just the islands,' said Macleod. 'I was looking at the religious spaces where all the chapels were.'

'What were you doing that for? What case made that come up?'

'It wasn't a case. It was part of a thing I was doing with the church,' said Macleod.

'Perry says holy ground, too. He says in the book it talks about it being holy ground. The sacrificial site.'

'Well, then,' said Macleod. 'One with a chapel on it.'

'You said there could be lots of them. There could be lots of—'

'You have a name, and you want to see on a map if there's something holy there. If there're chapels or religious sites. You need to cross-reference. Phone Ross! Nobody cross-references better than Ross.'

'You're right,' said Hope. 'You're right.' She closed down the call and looked back at Perry. He was still engrossed in the book.

'It's all here,' he said. 'It's all here. We just need to find the place.'

Hope was already dialling up Ross's number.

'This is Ross.'

'You got an internet connection there?'

'Yes,' he said.

'Right, don't argue, don't comment, just do, please,' said Hope. 'We need this quick. I need to know if there's an Eilean Mòr, Gaelic—'

'Big island,' said Ross, and Hope wondered, was she the only one unaware of this?

'I need an Eilean Mòr on the west coast with a chapel on it.'

'Why do you—'

'Don't,' said Hope. 'Do it, fast. I've got a life that depends on it.'

'Okay,' said Ross.

Hope stood in silence, looking out at the now-dark water ahead of her. Night was closing in. Is that when they would do it? Had they already done it?

As she stood there and waited, she thought about asking Ross was he getting close, but she knew better. That was the thing about Ross; he was methodical. You gave him the problem, and he would just work through it. He wouldn't come back to you if he didn't have anything. If Ross had come up with something, even if it was only a possibility, he'd be on that phone. She heard the car door close behind her, and Perry came over.

'Have we got—'

'Shh,' said Hope. 'Ross is looking up things for me.'

'Been thinking,' whispered Perry in her ear. 'This book, this talks about McGrubbin. McGrubbin has written about all these people underneath her. I'm not sure McGrubbin's written or knows about anybody above her. If this is a secret group, if this is a cult, for want of a better word, or an organisation, they will not be known to her, all of them. That's how they work, isn't it? Keep your connections simple, so you can cut one off. I don't know if we'll be going higher from this.'

'What do you mean? Surely the group knows, the group who's coming after them, these people who want to kill them?'

'Not necessarily. If you knew that, if you knew all the way up, why wouldn't you just kill them, quietly? Why do it like this?'

'So people know,' said Hope.

'Who knows,' said Perry. 'The public? The public hasn't got a clue what's going on here. Ordinary people don't know that there's a group in the past which carried out arbitrary acts of execution. The public don't know. These books being delivered with the bodies is for us.

'Why? Why would you do this with Macleod? You would keep Macleod out of it,' said Perry. 'You wouldn't want him investigating because he would come after you. If you knew all these people who were in this society, if you knew the people that actually did it, all the way up to the top, just kill them. Round them up. Take them to one side. Execute them. Disappear. That's your vengeance.

'Otherwise, get your evidence and put it up on TV. Don't bring in somebody like Macleod. After all, why would you bring in Macleod except to find things out? He's a detective like us. We discover stuff. This is only the start,' said Perry. 'It must run deeper. This must be one arm of many. And they want Macleod to go through it all and clear out.'

'But why not just come to him?' asked Hope. 'Why not just—'

'Did they already? This wasn't their first contact, was it? The first contact,' said Perry, 'was whatever happened with Emmett. Macleod put Emmett onto that. There must have been contact. They've tried to stir his feelings. Now they're giving him bodies. What makes Macleod react more than anything?'

Hope looked at him, feeling chilled.

'Hope. Hope. It's Alan.' She stared back at her phone.

'Go ahead. I'm right here,' said Hope to Ross on the phone.

'I got it. Eilean Mòr with a chapel. I've got it. It's up by Craob Haven.'

'Craob Haven! Craob Haven! Perry,' said Hope. 'Car. Craob Haven! Let's go!'

Chapter 23

'That's nearly a three-hour drive,' said Perry. 'We need to get some units there quicker than that.'

'We must have a helicopter somewhere near here who can get us down.' Hope placed a call to Susan Cunningham, who was at the search hub.

'Have you got a helicopter anywhere?' she asked. 'Somewhere close to Mallaig. I need a lift. Mallaig to Craob Haven. We believe the site's down there. Eilean Mòr. It's got a chapel on it. Ross has found it.'

'That far down? Most of the units are up round Mallaig. It's a big search area. We didn't think of going down there. Craob Haven's well known. It's got a marina. There's plenty of people walking about. They haven't reported any motorboats come in there.'

'They may have been hiding out. Have you got a helicopter that can get me down there?'

'Wait a minute. Yes, yes I have,' said Susan. 'I'll start getting units going that way as well.'

'I don't want to scare these people off. So if anything gets there, tell them not to arrive with flashing lights. More low key. But it'll be on the island. Probably not in Craob Haven itself.'

'Helicopter will be with you in two minutes.'

'Okay, I'll be taking Perry down with me. Let Macleod know. Tell him that Perry thinks this might be the endgame. If we don't find her . . . well, he's not sure there's going to be more killings like this. He thinks the trail's going to die.'

'Why's he think that?' asked Susan.

'No time to explain. Just pass it on, and then get yourself up that way.'

'That's quite far out. It's Lochgilphead, isn't it?'

'Yes,' said Hope. But already the helicopter could be heard. She saw it fly in low, and land out towards the road. Perry had anticipated it and ran out to make sure no cars were there. Thankfully, Mallaig was quiet at the moment.

Hope zipped up her leather jacket, ran over to the helicopter, and jumped into the rear with Perry. He had stuck one of the large police jackets on, which was always an improvement for Perry.

Perry liked to wear a suit jacket, loose and open. It was never useful if you were out in the middle of the night and cold. Susan had berated him many a time about putting on a proper police jacket. He seemed to be getting the idea.

Hope liaised with the pilot, advising she wanted to set down at Eilean Mòr, beside Craob Haven. Not Craob Haven, but the island. Hope told them to get going. As they lifted into the air, her nausea was there again. She put her hand over her mouth.

'You okay?' asked Perry. 'Let me take the lead on this.'

She forced the bile back down her throat. 'Perry, focus. Don't worry about me. Focus. We have to get them.'

The helicopter raced through the night sky and Hope watched as the water and the west coast passed beneath them.

Lights of the towns shone, little beacons in the dark, but it wasn't long before they arrived at Craob Haven.

'Where do you need me to set down?' asked the pilot.

Hope had her phone out, looking at Eilean Mòr and the chapel on a map. 'It's over there,' she said. 'Swing low across there.'

The pilot went down to approximately five hundred feet. As he got closer, Perry suddenly shouted, 'Motorboat, motorboat, at the island! It's at the island!'

'Land there,' said Hope. 'Anywhere on that island. Just get it down on that island.'

She looked across at Perry, who turned to her. 'I've got this,' he said. 'Let me take the lead.'

Like hell, Hope thought. *I'll get them.*

The pilot swung in low over the water, setting down on the edge of the island. It wasn't big, but he was at the far end of the island from the motorboat. There was a broken-down chapel in the middle, and standing outside it, Hope could see three figures in the dark. One was standing aloof, while another had his arm around the throat of a woman. It must have been McGrubbin. In one hand, the man held a knife. They stared and watched as Hope jumped out of the helicopter.

'Police!' she shouted. 'Stand down! Police! Don't touch that woman!'

Perry was out of the helicopter now too, shouting, and Hope ran forward. There were several hundred yards between them and the perpetrators of the would-be execution. Hope yelled, trying to lift her voice above the noise of the rotor blades of the helicopter. She stared in horror as the figure holding McGrubbin swung a blade around in the air. The arm was then brought down, and the other arm removed from around McGrubbin's throat, the hand now instead gripping the shoulder. It was almost like a dream, or rather a nightmare. Hope continued to charge.

She was here; she was ready to stop this, but they weren't listening. There was a quick slash, and she saw the blood pour from the neck. Hope was not squeamish, but currently the bile was running up and down her throat because of her pregnant state, the nausea threatening to overcome her.

She tripped and stumbled, falling to the ground and onto her knees, and then, against all her efforts, she vomited. It took a moment to shake her head, to clear her vision again. She looked up from the mess in front of her, and from her kneeling position, she saw McGrubbin's body being allowed to tumble to the ground. One man threw a book down in a zippy bag as they turned to run.

Perry had gone well, though, racing across the ground. He'd got close to the site, close enough that when the men ran, he was able to close on one, but was clearly slower.

Hope got herself back to her feet, ran as she watched Perry dive out and flick the ankles of one man. One of his feet collided with the other, and the man toppled over, rolling onto the ground. Perry was up like a shot and then jumped on the man. Hope ran hard. They had one but she could see the other man, the one who had committed the execution. He had stopped, no longer running to the motor launch but now turning back to his colleague.

He still had the sacrificial knife in his hands. The weapon that had slit the throat of McGrubbin. There wasn't a lot between Perry and the knife wielder. But Hope was also getting closer. Her guts roared, but she raced as hard as she could across the uneven ground.

She skipped past a couple of stones and saw Perry with his back to the man with the knife.

'Perry!' she shouted as hard as she could. 'The other one!'

She saw Perry turn as the knife was brought down upon him. He flung his arms up and blocked it, enough for the man to stumble and the swing to have missed.

Hope was now fifteen feet away. She ran hard and flung herself at the man, hitting him with her shoulder and sending him sprawling.

The attacker that Perry had felled, however, was now getting back up, mainly because Perry had spun to protect himself from the knife. This meant the other man had got up and as Perry turned back to him, he was punched solidly across the jaw, sending him sprawling backwards.

Hope was recovering her feet, and the man with the knife was now standing directly opposite her. He stepped forward, slashing wildly with the blade. Hope stepped inside, drove her elbow up and in towards his head, causing the man to spin round to the ground. But as he did so, she was hit from the side by the other man. He pulled her down to the ground, climbing on top of her.

'You get the bitch,' the man spat at his colleague. Hope was aware that his colleague, who had received the attentions of her elbow, was getting back up with the knife.

But Perry was back up on his feet as well. He looked groggy, but he was taking his jacket off, wrapping it up around his arm now. She saw the man stab at Perry a couple of times, but Perry wrapped the jacket around the man's hand. He got close before the man kicked him in the stomach, and then followed it up with another kick that made Perry stumble all the way back.

The time bought by Perry allowed Hope to wriggle out from the man holding her tipping him onto the side. Trying to get up onto her feet, she found her leg grabbed, and once again tumbled back to the ground. She could taste the bile in her mouth, the sick that had already come, and spat. She was empty, drained. Dammit, she wasn't as fit as she should be.

As she went to get back up, she felt an elbow catch her on the side of the chin, pummelling her back down. But the man above her then shouted, 'Grab that knife, let's go!'

Hope took a moment to recover, trying to breathe in any amount of air to fill her lungs again. She rolled on the ground, hearing the footsteps of the others running away. Looking up, she saw they were making for the motorboat. As she stood up, she looked down at Perry. He was breathing heavily, winded, and he wasn't getting up any time soon. A quick glance saw a lifeless McGrubbin. Should Hope go to her? Last chance, Perry had said. This could be the close. This could be it.

Hope turned and ran as hard as she could after the men.

The motorboat was in the water, close to the island but it wasn't beached. It was too big a vessel for that and they'd obviously chosen somewhere they could get close. The men were splashing in through the water. The helicopter was lifting and shining a spotlight on the launch. Hope also thought she saw another figure in the darkness to her right, running along the shoreline. She couldn't be sure, and she didn't care, because her focus was on the two men running for the motorboat.

One jumped on board, turned round, and put his hand out for the second. They were almost in up their waist when they were climbing on board. Hope hit the water. It was cold, and she could feel the chill almost instantly soaking through her jeans.

They were pregnancy jeans. Smart looking, but slightly bigger, and the fabric was softer. It meant the cold came in all the quicker. She'd heard the motorboat engines fire up. Hope strode as hard as she could, breathless. Hope grabbed the back end of the motorboat as it started to pull away.

She felt the tug of the water pulling her back to it but she got a second hand up on the side of the vessel and was clinging onto a rope. There were several outriggers along the side, floats to keep the boat clear of a jetty, but right now they were providing handholds for Hope. She pulled hard, lifting herself from the water as the motorboat sped up. After placing a leg onto one of the outriggers, Hope flung herself up and over, rolling onto the deck.

She tried to get up onto her feet, the boat rolling this way and that. It was a large enough boat, and there was clearly a below deck, from which someone was emerging. Hope stood up, exhausted, almost wild eyed and tried to run forward. The man she was going towards simply stepped to one side and hit her with something across the back of the head. She fell hard onto the deck.

* * *

Perry eventually rolled up onto his knees. He felt like his guts had been kicked out of the back of him. He was scrambling for breath. A glance over and he saw the blood around a woman's face. McGrubbin.

Perry stared and saw Hope getting on to the motorboat as it pulled away. Stumbling across, heading towards where it had been in the water, he saw the helicopter with the spotlight tailing that motorboat. He arrived at the beach side and looked at the water before him. The trail of the motorboat was slowly disappearing, its wake dissipating.

'Hope,' he said involuntarily. She had a little one with her. She shouldn't be out there. This was his task. He should be there. Perry could feel his body shaking. He wasn't sure what to do. Needed help. The helicopter should call it in, shouldn't it? The helicopter pilot should get the distress going. Get people out. Perry looked at the water in front of him before turning and looking at the scene behind him. He felt absolutely useless.

Chapter 24

ope's head pounded. The bile was back in her throat, and she wasn't sure how long she'd been out for. It couldn't have been that long, could it? She could still hear the engines of the motorboat working hard through the water. However, she couldn't feel the air, the chilly night air that had been in her lungs. Yet her legs, they were cold.

Not surprising. The jeans were stuck to them, still very damp. No, she couldn't have been out for that long. She opened one eye and could see the floor in front of her. She was in a cabin, she thought. Maybe I'm down below in the motorboat.

Hope was lying on her front, but her hands were behind her back, and she could feel them tied together. She went to struggle with her feet, but they were tied as well at the ankles. Hope remembered clambering onto the boat. She remembered coming at the people, but she had been struck. It had been so much of an effort, and this morning sickness, it had taken so much out of her. She hadn't been on full steam.

Perry. Perry was all right, though. She gave a smile at that, and then she thought of McGrubbin. The woman was dead. She remembered the slash across the throat along with the blood.

Hope had not seen many people killed in her lifetime. She'd seen lots of dead people, because that was the job, but actually killed in front of her, that was rare. Thank God for that. She lay there, wondering about what had just happened. She remembered a figure on the edge, on the periphery of her vision, as she'd run for the boat.

Where would the boat go now? They had her on board. Why? They'd kept her, tied her up. Why? Why not just throw her off the back? Of course I've seen them, haven't I? I'd got close. Or maybe they would use her, in case they were boarded, in case the helicopter had kept track.

She didn't know. How many minutes had it been? Half an hour? An hour? A few minutes? Hope tried to relax, but that was difficult when her hands were tied behind her back, and she was struggling to move her feet. She heard a door open and tried to look around. There were feet now, in the cabin.

'I don't—' Hope started, but a hand went over her mouth.

'Now, now, let's not get too mouthy for a police officer. They don't know I'm here, but they know you're here, and we don't want them to come down and see me, because if they do, the game could be up.'

For a moment, Hope thought it was Kirsten, but then realised voice was wrong. *Completely wrong. And would Kirsten have called her a police officer? Kirsten would call her by rank. She'd been in the force. Or she would just call her Hope.*

Who was this person?

'It's a little awkward, the situation at the moment,' said the woman. 'You see, you've nearly got them. So very close. We've got the helicopter following but these people, they don't deserve public scrutiny. These people need to be dispatched.

Need to be kept quiet.'

Is this one of Anna Hunt's mob? thought Hope. The hand over her mouth was lifted. Hope took in a deep breath.

'Has Anna sent you?'

'Anna?' said the woman. The voice was husky. 'No, not Anna.' Hope could feel the bonds holding her hands together being removed, and then the bonds on her feet were cut.

'Easy, gently, okay. You're going to help me, because you're an exemplary officer. These people need to be stopped before the next killing spree they'll go on. You're a good officer, you know that. Sometimes things have to be not done quietly, as much as we love our law system. Doesn't always work for everyone. Sometimes people play above the law, and you have to silence them rather more quietly.

'They're making an awful lot of noise at the moment. So, you and I are going to creep up. We're going to despatch this lot, and then you're going to go ashore. You're a hero. Oh, don't worry. It won't be you that's killed them. The boat will sink, but we'll make sure there's enough evidence for you to take away once it's done. But you can say it's over. You've solved the case. It's all wrapped up.'

Hope rolled onto her back and looked up into the face of a woman of maybe forty. She was strong, though. Very strong. She had a mask around her mouth, a simple scarf, but there were no shades on, and the eyes were piercing into Hope. Were they trying to judge if Hope was going to play along?

Well, will I? thought Hope. *I don't have much option. They're up top. The woman's here. If I don't go with her, she'll likely knock me out again and get rid of me if I don't fit her formula. The other option is, try and take her out here, and then stop the others. On my own. I'm not sure I could do either.*

'Okay,' said Hope. 'We stop them. I don't know how your plan's going to work. You're going to have to fill me in on that one.'

'Good,' said the woman. 'You understand. Don't worry. We have friends who can make things work. Macleod won't know a thing. You just have to play your part. I'm sure you can play against him, can't you?'

Rather than nod furiously, Hope let her face become a muddle for a moment, before then agreeing. She thought it was more authentic. Hope would never desperately agree to something. She needed to sell the idea she was in on the plan, reluctantly. But if she could get up and stop the other three, then maybe she could stop this woman. Or at least wave in the helicopter if it was still following.

The woman helped Hope up to her feet, and they tiptoed to the cabin door.

'This one leads out to another door,' said the woman. 'From there, we're able to get up to the bridge. It's not that high up. Not a lot of room to manoeuvre. There's three of them. Very strong. I'm sure a woman of your talents can handle it, though.'

Hope watched as the woman removed a knife from inside of her clothing.

'Sorry, I don't have one for you,' she said. 'I'll make quick work of them with this.' The woman opened the door in front of them, gently. There were dulled cabin lights on down below, but the boat was still bouncing about, roaring through the sea, and Hope could hear the helicopter up above.

There was still another door to go through. They stole over to it, quickly, and then the woman pulled the door back. Hope, however, saw a knife on the side of the small cabin and grabbed it, causing the other woman to smile. It was ornate and still had blood on the blade. Hope tucked it inside her jeans.

The woman was dressed in black, almost entirely. It was no wonder she had been difficult to see. Hope reckoned it must have been the same person moving in the shadows before she got onto the boat, but whatever, it didn't matter. She was here, and this was Hope's chance to escape.

'Can you take all three, or do you want me to—'

The woman put a finger up to her lips. She crept forward through the door and then came back quickly.

'There's one up on the wheel. You could get the nearest one.'

That must mean that the woman was going to take two of them out. Hope was impressed. She'd have to move quickly. The woman had seen the layout, while Hope hadn't, and would go the furthest.

The woman opened the door. Hope crept out, and they made their way up some narrow but tall stairs before peering over the top of them. Hope could see the man at the wheel and two others looking around.

'What are we going to do with her?' said one.

'Best just to die. Maybe we should dump her. Too complicated, otherwise.'

'Well, this was it, anyway. We don't have to worry. Maybe we should dump her. That'll have Macleod investigating, won't it? That's what he wanted. Him on the job.'

'Just keep going,' said a voice. 'We've got to outrun that bloody helicopter.'

The helicopter was up above, the whirring sound almost deafening down at the bridge. They shouted as they spoke to each other but Hope awaited a signal from the woman beside her. She gave Hope a tap on the shoulder, pointed her fingers forward, and then pulled her elbow down sharply to indicate a 'go'.

The woman was up the last of the steps and in before Hope had even moved. Hope could see the woman had engaged the middle one of the men, whereas the one who was closest to the steps was trying to come over to assist his colleague. Hope was able to grab him before he saw her, pulling his shoulder and throwing him across the boat.

He slammed hard into the side, and Hope looked forward to the man on the wheel. He looked terrified, panicked, and then she saw him flick up a plastic panel. There was a red switch there.

It was only a split second, but the thought tore through Hope's mind.

The boat's rigged. It made sense. Get into trouble. Blow it up. Destroy as much evidence as possible.

Hope took a step. Then another. A foot up by the rail of the boat. And she flung herself, for all she was worth, out into the pitch-black sea. She crashed into it, feeling the cold water around her.

The boat continued on. The helicopter still there too. Hope surfaced, putting her arms out with her legs, trying to float, trying not to let the shock of the water take over. As she lay back, she heard the deafening explosion. The boat was ripped apart. Hope fought to keep the blinding light from stopping her from seeing anything once it had gone.

There were little bits of flaming wreckage on the water, but the boat had well and truly been blown to smithereens.

Hope could feel the ritual knife she'd picked up still inside her pregnancy jeans. Now she needed to rouse some attention. She was out in the water, and getting cold. Surely somebody would come, but she'd need to stay afloat, need to stay afloat until then.

She thought about the little one inside her. She'd need to keep going, keep going for that wee one. Hope lay back, floating as best she could, and heard the helicopter circling round and round. It was then she saw the searchlight; it was pointing down at her. She tried to wave, but the helicopter didn't come any closer. It kept up high, but it kept the beam on her.

Hope must have been in the water for another ten minutes. She was okay, though the cold was seeping in. Maintaining her position, she kept floating and tried to remain calm. She was an excellent swimmer, always had been. But you couldn't swim in from here. You would be exhausted and die from that. Instead, she heard a boat crashing through the water.

She saw lights being pointed at her.

'Are you okay?' cried a voice over the helicopter. 'Are you all right?'

'Yes,' said Hope. 'Yes!'

A lifeboat pulled up beside her, the crew hauling her on board. 'I'll take you back in. There'll be some ambulances over by Craob Haven. We'll get over to the marina.' Hope was lying back with a foil blanket wrapped around her.

'I'm good,' she said. 'I'm good.'

'How many people were on that boat?'

'Me and four others that I know of,' said Hope.

'Did you see anyone else survive the explosion? Anybody else in the water?' the man asked.

'Not that I'm aware of.'

She could feel herself shivering now. Was she becoming hypothermic? Whatever, the coastguard was racing back to the land. Craob Haven Marina was the destination, and as the boat pulled up, Hope could see several helicopters had landed in the distance. She was looking at people she didn't recognise. They weren't in police uniforms. There were police there, and she saw Perry.

'Quick, let's get you inside an ambulance,' said a coastguard. The crewmen helped her walk ashore and put her straight into the back of an ambulance. Inside was a paramedic, dressed in green, with long black hair. They had shades on, which Hope thought strange but she lay down on the bed.

'I've got it,' said the paramedic, and shooed everyone else out of the vehicle, closing the doors behind her.

'You got anything?' said a voice Hope recognised. The shades went up, and she looked into the face of Kirsten Stewart.

'What do you mean?' asked Hope.

'They're going to come in. They're going to frisk you. If you've got anything, any evidence, whatever, that you need me to take away. Give it now.'

Hope pushed down the pregnancy jeans, and the knife fell out, its ornate handle and deadly blade. Kirsten grabbed it.

'I'll just get somebody to deal with you,' she said. 'See you around.' She stepped out of the ambulance.

Hope could hear a kerfuffle. Somebody was asking to go into the ambulance and getting told no, then getting told yes. Soon, several official-looking people had come in, including two men that Hope had thought were almost heavies.

'We just need to check what you've got on you,' said a woman.

She went through Hope's coat, pulled out her ID, pulled out her wallet, and pulled out everything else that was in her pockets. When they were satisfied they'd been through it all, Hope was frisked, and they left. A paramedic jumped into the ambulance.

'I don't know what that was about,' he said. 'I couldn't get past them. Sorry, are you all right? My other colleague said you were probably hypothermic. Let's check you over.'

Hope lay back, letting the man do his work. He was joined by another colleague shortly. And then she heard a voice.

'Is she okay? She's pregnant. You need to know that. She's pregnant.'

'I can tell them that myself, Perry.'

'Can I come in?' Perry said to the paramedics. Hope saw the nod and Perry came up and over to her.

'You okay? Did you get hurt at all?'

'A few smacks around the face,' said Hope. 'Other than that, I'm good. I'm good.'

'Sorry,' said Perry. 'Should have been me there.'

'Don't be daft,' she said. 'You okay? You took quite a kick.'

'I'm fine,' said Perry. He leaned over and kissed Hope on the forehead. 'I'm glad you're all right.' She was going to say something, because he was like a mothering hen. But she let it go. The man had helped. The man was looking out for her. Always.

Hope was in the ambulance for an hour or so, before being taken to the hospital. In Glasgow, she was kept in a separate room and she wasn't sure who was standing outside. They weren't police officers, not even police officers in plain uniforms. But there was little she could do, and she lay back, trying to focus on her recovery. There was a knock at the door. It opened, and she saw the fedora hat first, and then the long jacket.

'You two can go.' A man stuck his head in and looked at Macleod. 'I mean it, you can go. Tell Anna Hunt, thank you very much, but you can go.' One looked at the other, and then they disappeared.

'Sorry,' said Macleod.

'Seoras, I need to tell you something—'

Macleod looked and saw that one man hadn't quite left. He put up his hand, showing Hope to stay quiet.

Macleod watched until the door of the room was closed again. He then sat down, still holding up his hand. After a couple of minutes, he went outside, and Hope could hear him tell somebody that he said they could go. He went through the routine again, five minutes later, popping his head outside. Only then did he come up beside her bed.

'I got something. End of the line, Perry said, but I got something. I got—'

'Never mind, never mind what happened to it, or whatever you've got, you just get better. Yes, the little one's okay, I take it?'

'I think so, they'll check me, no doubt.'

'You just focus on getting better, and we'll get you back up the road,' said Macleod loudly. 'Definitely the end of the line,' he repeated. 'We're done with this one.'

Chapter 25

You don't normally call people in on a Sunday morning,' said Hope. She'd been back up only a couple of days after a brief stay in the Glasgow hospital. In truth, she'd hoped for a morning of quietness and solitude, with only John's arms for company. Still, when Macleod had messaged, it was half past four in the morning, and the Inverness station was quiet.

Macleod had advised Hope to come in but park her car elsewhere, and not in the station car park. She'd climbed the stairs, seeing next to no one before making her way to his office. Once inside, she realised that his main lights weren't on. Just a small one—a desk lamp in the corner. It gave the room an eerie glow.

Macleod was sitting behind his desk, and he had three seats sitting before it. They were empty when Hope arrived. However, in true Macleod fashion, there was a cafetière of coffee and he poured a cup as she sat down.

'This is all a bit cloak and dagger, isn't it?' said Hope.

'You see, that's why I like you,' said Macleod. 'Clarissa would have asked me what the hell is going on. You don't. Instead, you ask that question much more subtly.'

'I do still wonder what's going on, though,' said Hope.

'This case—you did well.' He handed the coffee over to her. 'It's decaf. I thought it best due to the little one, although I struggled. Anyway, you did extremely well. I was advised from above that things are okay. They will not tell the public how McGrubbin was involved. Though they say she's thought to be the head of the group that died.'

'Well, that's probably not that far from the truth, though there's maybe more than one group.'

'The boat that was blown up, they did a good job on it. Some pieces were found, but they've been taken aside. I can't get access to a lot of things. It's been said that there was foreign involvement, and we need to keep things quiet. Higher than my pay grade,' said Macleod.

'Did you raise merry hell at that?' asked Hope. 'It's what you would do.'

'I did,' said Macleod, 'though I knew I wouldn't get anywhere. But yes, I kicked hard. It didn't do any good. Things got taken over from us by a higher level. But apparently all's good. They say the case is closed. There's no need to have us on it anymore. This foreign element meant things needed to be wrapped up more quietly. Interesting, though. I spoke to Anna Hunt. They didn't ask her to keep anything quiet. They didn't talk to her at all.'

'Oh. She will not be pleased with that.'

'No, she wasn't. Not at all.'

'So, is that it?' asked Hope. 'We just call it a day? Let somebody else take it on?'

'I wouldn't say that.'

There was a rap at the door. Macleod advised the caller to come in and Hope saw Emmett. He was in jeans and t-shirt with some barbarian looking at her from his chest.

'Thanks for coming in,' said Macleod. Emmett simply nodded, sat down, and allowed Macleod to pour him a coffee.

'Have you read everything from Hope's team?' asked Macleod.

Emmett nodded. 'They've closed it all off. The report, it clearly ties into a lot of what I was investigating, but I don't understand where we're going now. This faction, this group,' said Emmett, 'who want us to reveal something—they don't seem to have much more. Don't seem to know how much higher to go.'

'That's what Perry said,' said Hope looking at Emmett. 'Perry said that this was the endgame, because we got nothing. Nowhere else to go. They wanted us to reach up higher.'

'I can understand that,' said Emmett. 'He's probably right.'

'The problem is,' said Macleod, 'the people who have perpetrated the original crimes—those who killed Isbister, those who set this all up, who took out the MacIntoshes down in Glasgow, the ones that the other group are trying to expose— they think they've closed it off. You said you spoke to a woman on that boat, and she gave you a lecture.'

'A lecture? She told me how I could cover something up from you. She obviously doesn't know you.'

Macleod gave a faint smile, but then his serious face came back. 'Problem is, we have nothing up above to go on,' he said. 'It looks like what Perry said is true. I spoke to Anna Hunt, and she agreed. It seems to be that McGrubbin was the head of a branch. Beneath her was our smartly dressed man. Still trying to get a handle on him and his name. Below him was our civic leader, Funnell.

'Now his family aren't daft either. They've been covering

up like anything, too. And below him was poor Peter and Barraclough. It looks like Peter was the way this revenge group broke in. I think that's how they got hold of everything. That was the line of attack. And they unravelled it. Similar to the way we are.

'But they led us through and got us through to where they got to. And I think they were hoping for us to get more. Thing is, to get more we'd have to dig something else up.'

'Somebody came in and took the one thing we had,' said Hope.

'What does she mean?' asked Emmett.

'It's not in the report,' said Macleod, 'but Hope got away with a ritual knife. At least, that's how she described it. A ritual knife. One that was used to kill McGrubbin and possibly the rest. But without Jona getting hold of it, we haven't been able to ascertain that.'

'But where is it, then?' said Emmett.

'A paramedic took it off me when I was in the ambulance after jumping off the boat into the water. I thought it was Kirsten,' said Hope. 'It was Kirsten, wasn't it? I wasn't just delirious or something.'

Macleod reached down into a drawer of his desk. He pulled it open, lifted an item out, and put it on the table. It had a long blade and on the end of it was a wooden handle with elements carved into it.

'This isn't here,' said Macleod. 'This was never recovered. Nobody picked up anything. You got off that boat, Hope, with nothing, as you stated in your report.'

'Of course, silly me,' said Hope.

'So, this knife, what do we know about it?' asked Emmett. 'Can we go down this line of attack?'

'We can,' said Macleod. 'Until an hour ago, this knife was in the hands of a certain Asian forensic officer doing some late-night study for exams. At least that's what her team thought. She's confirmed to me it's her distinct belief that this knife was used to kill our victims.'

'The same one?' said Emmett. 'For them all?'

'Certainly, the same type of knife. Possibly the same one.'

'That makes it ritualistic to use the same one. I mean, there was no need. You could have slit their throats with anything,' said Hope.

'It's also got markings on it,' said Emmett. 'That's a knife with history. If you wanted to keep things covered up, you certainly wouldn't use that one. People would know. Find out. Be able to trace it.'

'You'd think, wouldn't you?' said Macleod. He reached forward and picked up his own coffee and drank it.

'I'll take it,' said Emmett. 'I'll take it and run with it. See what I can come up with.'

'No, you won't,' said Macleod. 'You absolutely won't.'

'You want me to do it?' asked Hope. 'What do I know about ornate knives? It would look suspicious if I've done this case and I'm then running around looking for a knife, not based on anything else.'

Macleod stood up. 'There's no way I would let you go running around on this again. You're not fit for it.' Hope raised her eyebrows at him. 'You're struggling with the morning sickness. Perry told me. And before you start, he's not being a mothering, coddling, busybody. He's right.'

'So what?' asked Hope. 'You're going to do it?'

'I can't do it,' said Macleod. 'They know me. The people at the top of this who want to cover everything up, who are perpetrators of previous crimes that this group carried out, murders someone else is now trying to highlight—they know me. And if I get involved in any of it, they'll trace it, they'll get worried, and they'll take much more serious action. Until I know exactly what's happened, what's gone on, and how deep it is, I don't wish to poke the lion.'

'So what?' said Hope. 'We sit back? We do nothing?'

'No,' said Macleod. 'That's not what we do. They've seen Emmett. They've seen you. And they know me. Any of us start doing investigations into something, and they'll be on to us. Any of your team try to do it on the quiet, they'll be on to them. They'll be looking for them. However, one thing they do trust is my sensibilities. There's no more evidence, as far as they're concerned. Nothing for me to investigate. So, this one will be done on the quiet. And it will be done by somebody they don't know. Somebody who hasn't been involved so far.'

'Who?' asked Hope. 'Who are you going to pull in? It's a murder inquiry.'

There was a knock at the door. It opened, and a woman dressed in tartan trews and with a shawl wrapped around her, closed the door stared. First at Hope, then at Emmett, and then over at Macleod.

'What the bloody hell's this?' she said. 'Staff meetings at this time of the morning?'

'If we can use the voice we don't normally use. The quiet one,' said Macleod.

'Don't you even start being cheeky to me,' said Clarissa. And then she stopped. There was no joviality in the air. 'What's up?' she asked.

'Come over here a minute,' said Macleod.

'Why?'

'I've made coffee,' said Macleod.

'You've made coffee for me before I've even got in. And you've got my two colleagues in here as well. Am I being set up?'

'Of course,' said Macleod. 'I need something from you.'

'What?' asked Clarissa.

'Look at this knife.' Clarissa's interest was now piqued, and she marched over to the desk. She picked up the knife, holding it in both hands, turning it over and over.

'Recognise it?'

'No,' she said. 'Not exactly. It's a ritual knife, though.'

'The blade?'

'It's a blade for killing. Like in an abattoir. Swiftly, quickly. No second chances. What's it got to do with me?' asked Clarissa.

'Here,' said Macleod, and he handed her a bunch of papers. 'Sit down and read.'

'You can tell me what it's about. Right here. I'm in front of your face. Yes.'

'No. I don't discuss it with you. Okay. Anything you get from me, there're no words uttered. Messages only.'

Clarissa looked up at him. She turned and looked at Hope, who simply gave her a nod, before Clarissa plonked herself down in the seat. It took her fifteen minutes to read everything through. Fifteen minutes, during which she only took two sips of coffee. Macleod, however, had finished two cups in this time.

'Okay,' said Clarissa, gingerly putting the paper back on Macleod's desk. 'What are you wanting from me? I've told you—it's a ritual knife. I don't know that much more beyond it.'

'It's quite simple,' said Macleod. 'I want you to find me where that knife comes from, why it's important, who's been using it. and where they acquired it from.'

'There are no receipts or anything with it.'

'I got it off the boat that blew up,' said Hope. 'We believe it was used in the killings.'

'Somebody used it for ritual killing. It's important. Why that knife? Where's it come from?'

'And I need you to do it quietly,' said Macleod. 'No antics. Proper quiet.'

'Why's Emmett here?' asked Clarissa.

'Because Emmett started this all off. There's more paper-work. But I don't want you to give anything away or to look with surprise, or non-surprise, if something is mentioned. And I want this done in the dark. Just you and Patterson.'

Clarissa stood up for a moment. 'Correct me if I'm wrong, but somebody blew a boat up that Hope was on. She barely got off with it with her life. Other people are running around, sacrificing people, left, right and centre. You won't even talk to me about what Emmett was doing, or how bad that was.'

'No,' said Macleod, 'but I should advise you that Emmett had a potshot taken at him.'

Clarissa smiled. 'You call me your Rottweiler, not your shield. I'm not here to creep around, and given what's been going on—you know I can handle myself to a point—but some of these people seem to be, well, more like professionals. This would seem to be something more suited to our Service.'

'No Service. No nothing. I want to get to the bottom of this. I want the people at the top who have perpetrated these crimes, and I want the people at the bottom who are trying to show them up by committing more. We work it through.'

'Okay,' said Clarissa, 'but we're going into dangerous places. I can't defend myself or Pats, like that.'

'Meet the third person of your team,' said Macleod.

Clarissa spun round. The far corner of the room moved. She thought there'd been a lot of coats there, but a couple dropped away and someone walked out. She was dressed in black trousers and a black jacket. The hair, long and black, hung down around her face.

'Remember me?' the woman asked Clarissa.

'Kirsten Stewart,' said Clarissa. 'Of course. I replaced you.'

'Well then, let's hope you're as good as me,' said Kirsten. Clarissa eyed her up and down and turned to Hope. 'Can she handle herself?'

'Handles herself better than any of us,' said Hope.

Clarissa turned round, put her hand out, and Kirsten shook it. 'Okay. Welcome on board,' said Clarissa. 'But just so you understand, I'm the boss.'

'No,' said Macleod. 'I'm actually the boss.'

'Never mind him,' said Clarissa. 'This is the arts world. I'm the boss. Let's get cracking.'

Read on to discover the Patrick Smythe series!

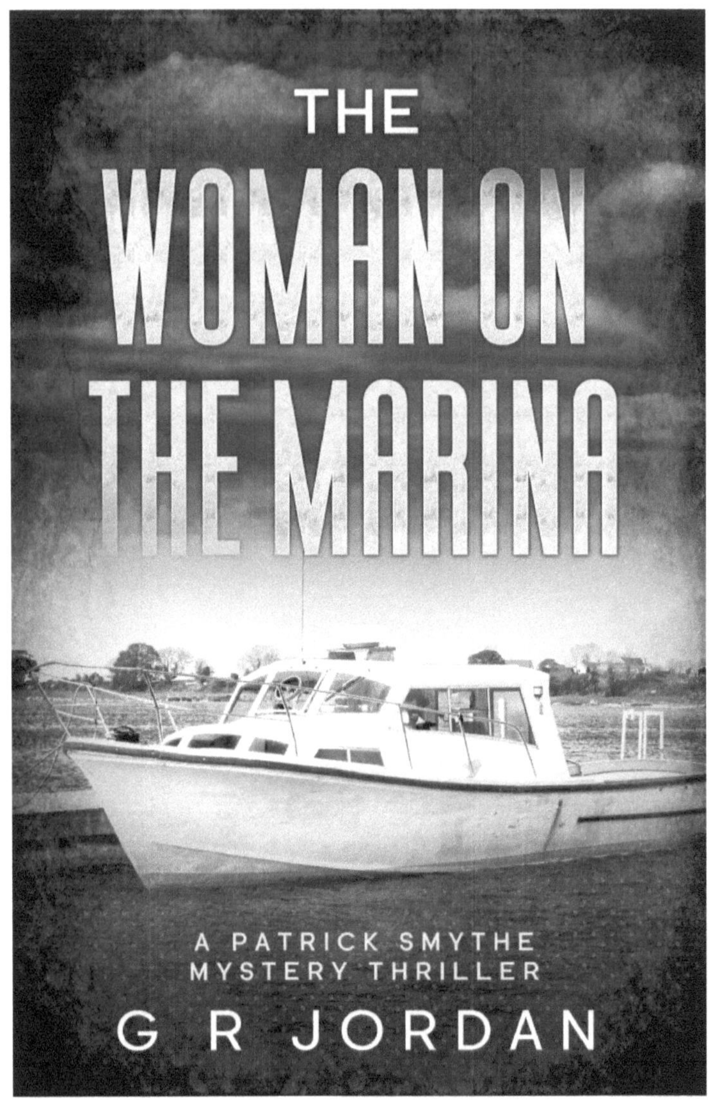
THE
WOMAN ON
THE MARINA
A PATRICK SMYTHE
MYSTERY THRILLER
G R JORDAN

Patrick Smythe is a former Northern Irish policeman who after suffering an amputation after a bomb blast, takes to the sea between the west coast of Scotland and his homeland to ply his trade as a private investigator. Join Paddy as he tries to work to his own ethics while knowing how to bend the rules he once enforced. Working from his beloved motorboat 'Craigantlet', Paddy decides to rescue a drug mule in this short story from the pen of G R Jordan.

Join G R Jordan's monthly newsletter about forthcoming releases and special writings for his tribe of avid readers and then receive your free Patrick Smythe short story.

Go to https://bit.ly/PatrickSmythe for your Patrick Smythe journey to start!

About the Author

GR Jordan is a self-published author who finally decided at forty that in order to have an enjoyable lifestyle, his creative beast within would have to be unleashed. His books mirror that conflict in life where acts of decency contend with self-promotion, goodness stares in horror at evil, and kindness blindsides us when we at our worst. Corrupting our world with his parade of wondrous and horrific characters, he highlights everyday tensions with fresh eyes whilst taking his methodical, intelligent mainstays on a roller-coaster ride of dilemmas, all the while suffering the banter of their provocative sidekicks.

A graduate of Loughborough University where he masqueraded as a chemical engineer but ultimately played American football, Gary had worked at changing the shape of cereal flakes and pulled a pallet truck for a living. Watching vegetables freeze at -40'C was another career highlight and he was also one of the Scottish Highlands "blind" air traffic controllers.

These days he has graduated to answering a telephone to people in trouble before telephoning other people to sort it out.

Having flirted with most places in the UK, he is now based in the Isle of Lewis in Scotland where his free time is spent between raising a young family with his wife, writing, figuring out how to work a loom and caring for a small flock of chickens. Luckily, his writing is influenced by his varied work and life experience as the chickens have not been the poetical inspiration he had hoped for!

You can connect with me on:

🌐 https://grjordan.com

📘 https://facebook.com/carpetlessleprechaun

Subscribe to my newsletter:

✉ https://bit.ly/PatrickSmythe

Also by G R Jordan

G R Jordan writes across multiple genres including crime, dark and action adventure fantasy, feel good fantasy, mystery thriller and horror fantasy. Below is a selection of his work. Whilst all books are available across online stores, signed copies are available at his personal shop.

Someone Else's Ritual (Highlands & Islands Detective Book 43)
https://grjordan.com/product/someone-elses-ritual
A hunt into history with a mysterious knife. Bloody tales of past deeds and a cult's modern agenda to match. Can DI Clarissa Urquhart uncover the trail of gory patriotism to release someone dear from the organisation's silent grip?

Handed a poisoned chalice, Macleod's Rottweiler must navigate the shadowy world of a society as brutal and deadly as it is immersed in the past. With a ritual knife that was openly used to kill members of the cult, Clarissa sets out to trace both sides in the recent murders. On a trail that goes far beyond her own shores, she has only the unflappable Pats and streetwise Kirsten Stewart for company. Will her guile and sheer bloodymindedness be enough to bring Macleod a solid link to the mysterious factions? Or will she end up a victim in someone else's ritual?

With all avenues closed, it's time to bring out your big guns!

Kirsten Stewart Thrillers

https://grjordan.com/product/a-shot-at-democracy

Join Kirsten Stewart on a shadowy ride through the underbelly of the Highlands of Scotland where among the beauty and splendour of the majestic landscape lies corruption and intrigue to match any city. From murders to extortion, missing children to criminals operating above the law, the Highland former detective must learn a tougher edge to her work as she puts her own life on the line to protect those who cannot defend themselves.

Having left her beloved murder investigation team far behind, Kirsten has to battle personal tragedy and loss while adapting to a whole new way of executing her duties where your mistakes are your own. As Kirsten comes to terms with working with the new team, she often operates as the groups solo field agent, placing herself in danger and trouble to rescue those caught on the dark side of life. With action packed scenes and tense scenarios of murder and greed, the Kirsten Stewart thrillers will have you turning page after page to see your favourite Scottish lass home!

There's life after Macleod, but a whole new world of death!

Jac's Revenge (A Jac Moonshine Thriller #1)

https://grjordan.com/product/jacs-revenge

An unexpected hit makes Debbie a widow. The attention of her man's killer spawns a brutal yet classy alter ego. But how far can you play the game before it takes over your life?

All her life, Debbie Parlor lived in her man's shadow, knowing his work was never truly honest. She turned her head from news stories and rumours. But when he was disposed of for his smile to placate a rival crime lord, Jac Moonshine was born. And when Debbie is paid compensation for her loss like her car was written off, Jac decides that enough is enough.

Get on board with this tongue-in-cheek revenge thriller that will make you question how far you would go to avenge a loved one, and how much you would enjoy it!

A Giant Killing (Siobhan Duffy Mysteries #1)

https://grjordan.com/product/a-giant-killing

A body lies on the Giant's boot. Discord, as the master of secrets has been found. Can former spy Siobhan Duffy find the killer before they execute her former colleagues?

When retired operative Siobhan Duffy sees the killing of her former master in the paper, her unease sends her down a path of discovery and fear. Aided by her young housekeeper and scruff of a gardener, Siobhan begins a quest to discover the reason for her spy boss' death and unravels a can of worms today's masters would rather keep closed. But in a world of secrets, the difference between revenge and simple, if brutal, housekeeping becomes the hardest truth to know.

The past is a child who never leaves home!